TWISTED THERAPIST

DOMINATING DESIRES
BOOK ONE

MAHI MISTRY

Twisted Therapist

Copyright © 2022 Mahi Mistry

All rights reserved. No part of this book may be reproduced or transmitted in any form or by any electronic or mechanical means, including information storage and retrieval systems, without written permission from the author, except for the use of brief quotations in a book review.

This book is a piece of fiction. Names, characters, places, and incidents are the product of the author's imagination. Any resemblance to actual events, locales, or persons, living or dead, is coincidental.

This book is licensed for your personal enjoyment only.
This book may not be re-sold or given away to other people. If you are reading this book and did not purchase it, or it was not purchased for your use only, then you should return it to the seller and purchase your own copy.
Thank you for respecting the hard work of this author.

Published by Mahi Mistry
Cover Design by GetCovers
ISBN e-Book: 978-93-5526-357-5
ISBN Paperback: 978-93-5526-522-7

Dedicated to Anastasia. You're a gem.

GET DIRTY WILD SULTAN FOR FREE

> He is my only chance at freedom.
> She is the daughter of my enemy.
> Will their love survive?

> "I am asking you to marry me."
> "Are you asking or ordering, Sultan?"
> "I am asking, Princess." I smiled at her.
> **"For now."**

To instantly receive Dirty Wild Sultan, a steamy royal romance with marriage of convenience, sign up for Mahi's Newsletter at mahimistry.com

1
YES, DAD

IVY

I was wet.

Completely soaked.

It had to rain today of all days. Maybe the weather reflected my emotions.

My finger pressed on the doorbell, wishing my brother would hurry. Wet puddles formed around my feet as cold water dripped down the tips of my dark hair, trailing down my face. I knew the mascara I had applied that morning was ruined, and my eyes were puffy and red.

"Hayden!" I sniffled, running a hand across my face and pressing the doorbell again and again. "Hurry, please!"

Stupid. I was so stupid. Maybe I deserved it for being such a naïve idiot.

Rain kept pattering around the porch, wetting the freshly cut grass. The scent of wet earth and grass gave me comfort as I stood outside my brother's house in San Diego. He had told me he would be here, hopefully with Zara, his fiancée, my best friend and Princess of Azmia, who was very pregnant. They were getting married in a couple of months in Azmia and wanted to visit and meet their friends and family.

I needed to hug my elder brother and hear him curse about stupid boys and coddle me like he always did whenever I was sad. I wanted to hear him talk about his work as a Navy Seal, about Azmia, and his life as a soon-to-be-Prince. Very fitting with our last name.

"Hayden!" I cried out, my voice thick. "Open up. Finally, I thought you'd—*oh*."

My lips parted as I came face to face with chiseled abs, water sluicing over each contour of the muscles. Rain muffled into the surroundings as I trailed my eyes over the chiseled chest, my mouth going dry. Licking my lips, I raised my eyes from strong collarbones, lick-worthy adam's apple, to sharp jaw, inviting lips to *very familiar* thundering grey colored orbs.

"*Petal*," he whispered, his eyes roving over my face, calling me with the nickname he had been using since he met me.

My eyes flickered down to the white towel wrapped around his waist, staying far too long on the perfect vee of his hipbones. The short trail of dark hair leading under the towel made me curious, creating an odd twinge of need between my legs and making my cheeks warm.

He is your brother's best friend, Ivy. Get your head out of those dirty fantasies.

But I couldn't. I had been crushing on his symmetrical face since the day he piggy backed me home and stayed with me until Hayden bandaged my bruised knee.

"Aiden." I licked my lips, my throat dry. "I didn't know you'd be here."

"I missed you..." His eyes softened before he noticed my soaked clothes and wrapped his large, warm hand around my arm, dragging me in. "Come inside, you will get cold."

I shivered, not from the cold, but from his touch as it singed through my skin. His eyes clouded when mine traveled over the muscles of his body—how the deltoids of his back clenched and unclenched when he pulled my suitcase inside. In just a towel.

I may or may not have checked out his ass, too.

With flaming cheeks, I looked away at the empty hallway filled with our picture frames on the wall. "Where's Hayden? I thought he would be home by now."

"He didn't tell you?" He said, his body closer to mine. "Zara got a flu so they will arrive next month."

I frowned, "Is Zara okay?"

"If it was serious, I'd know, Petal. Don't worry about it." Of course, he'd know. Besides being Hayden's best friend, he was a brilliant psychiatrist who helped a lot of soldiers and Navy Seal officers going through PTSD or more.

But hearing I wouldn't be able to meet my brother for a few more weeks made me sad. I tried to hide my disappointment and crossed my arms.

His stormy eyes fell on my chest, and he cleared his throat. "Stay here. I will bring you a towel."

He walked past me, straight towards the room, keeping the door ajar. I looked down at myself and cringed in horror. My nude bra was visible through the thin cotton top I had worn that morning, my cold nipples poking through the wet fabric.

I tried to cover them as much as I could with my long hair when Aiden came back, handing me the towel, his tall height looming over me. He had changed into a black tee —*boo*—and gray sweatpants, his feet bare. There was something odd about seeing him like that, with his damp hair sleeked back and the dim light creating shadows on his sharp face.

When I was young and he was in high school, I had always seen him wearing pants and shirts. After a couple of years, when I was in high school and he was busy with his work as a therapist, I rarely saw him in anything but crisp shirts and suits that stretched over his broad shoulders and pants that covered his long legs.

Aiden stepped closer, his hands gently patting my wet hair with a dry towel. He smelled so good. Of musky, sweet cologne and something sharp. I wanted to step closer and bury my face in his chest, take a long sniff and hug him.

But I didn't, because I didn't want to seem like a puppy.

His voice was low as he said, "I am staying here until I find a house nearby. I didn't know you would be back so soon from your university."

Right. The reason I was soaked with mascara running down my face and the constant ache in my heart.

Images of Jason in bed with Amanda flashed in my head, making my eyes burn and stomach heavy. Was I that naïve that I didn't know Jason was cheating on me for half of the year we had been in a relationship? Probably. Amanda, my friend and dorm mate, and Jason, my now-ex-boyfriend, used to hang out a lot, and I passed their relationship as platonic, trusting both of them.

I came back home with a suitcase as fast as I could.

"Yeah," I cleared my throat and looked down at my soaked *Spirited Away* socks, which Zara had bought for me. I felt like that. A wet sock. "Things happened and I…"

Shaking my head, I trailed off and peered up at him. "I never thought I'd meet you so soon."

His lips quirked. I knew after knowing him from years that it meant he was happy. "Me too." Stepping back, he said, "I… I had to leave Denver and come here."

I furrowed my brows at him and waited for him to say something more, but neither of us wanted to talk like that, standing in the hallway, after years of not meeting each other face-to-face.

I took a sharp breath when he tucked a wet lock of hair behind my ear. "I know he made you cry, Petal." His eyes hardened when he gazed at me as if he could read me like a poem. "But we will talk about what that shit did to you to make your cry after you take a hot shower."

I swallowed the lump in my throat, not able to meet his piercing eyes. I must be crazy to find his domineering tone hot. But my chest warmed hearing *that* tone. Aiden always used it with me to make me eat food on time when he was sleeping over at our house, telling me to be careful while I chopped onions and holding my hands under tap when I cut my finger, disapproving of my prom date and telling me not to go to the after party.

I wish I had listened to him because I had called *him*, not my brother, at two in the morning at the after party of the prom. Crying and asking him if he could pick me up. He had even given me his hoodie that I never returned and bought me ice cream at early morning.

He never once mocked me with his told-you-so look, just took care of me when I needed someone.

I didn't think he would enter my life once again when I got my heart broken by Jason.

"Yes, *Dad*," I teased, walking past him, his knuckles brushing my arm.

I shivered with goosebumps and hurried upstairs to my room when I felt him watching me. Hayden had insisted on having a room of my own in his house because he wanted me to visit him more. After leaving for Azmia, he had given me the keys, but I had lived at dorms to be more social.

Everything was still the same. With beige walls, a twin size bed in the corner with a metal head frame, white lace curtain surrounding the bed, fairy lights all over the walls hanging over Audrey Hepburn's poster, my half-empty closet, a vanity dresser with mirror and a bookshelf filled with fantasy books and my soft toys from childhood.

I trailed my finger over the picture frame of us three. Me,

my brother and Aiden when I was a kid. Being eleven years older than me, I didn't get to hang out with them a lot, but when I did, they treated me like their equal. I was smiling shyly at the camera because I was insecure about my braces at thirteen, my dark hair in two pigtails, my lilac dress flowing in the wind. Hayden was grinning, his blue-gray eyes as bright as the ocean behind us in the backdrop. My eyes averted to Aiden, the person I had been crushing on since I was six.

His eyes were clear, piercing gray, facing the camera with his face stern, his onyx hair tousled perfectly as if he had rolled out of the bed, a lock of hair falling over his forehead and touching his slashing dark brow. The corner of his lip curled just a little. He was amused and happy. I knew it even though some would think he looked bored. After knowing him for all these years, I knew he seemed happy at that moment. I glanced at his arm, his hand pressing against my shoulder, a friendly gesture, but it made my stomach flutter like it did when I was thirteen.

Stupid. That's what I was. Stupid and naïve that someone like him, like Aiden, would ever return the feelings I have been harboring inside me since we first met. He was smart and poised, treating his patients with kindness and being awarded for his voluntary work in hospitals. Being one of the best therapists in California, he was nothing short of a celebrity in his community. Compared to him, I was a twenty-one-year-old girl who got her heart broken because she couldn't see through Jason's sorry excuses.

I huffed and stripped out of my soaked clothes, heading straight to the ensuite bathroom. I would need a warm shower, some food and some alcohol to talk to, call my brother and have a chat with Aiden.

2

IT'S NOT GOING TO LICK ITSELF

AIDEN

There are times in my life that I wished I wasn't me, Aiden Stone. Like opening the door and seeing Ivy, my little petal, after such a long time. My first thought on seeing her was, *'It must be a dream.'* A very weird dream. Where her clothes were soaked, sticking to her curves like second skin, chocolate hair dripping with water, her bright blue eyes red and puffy, mascara running down her cheeks. My second thought was that she had been crying, and I wanted to do terrible things to the person who had made her cry.

When I was seventeen, I had watched her climb up a tree in the park, her eyes bright and grin wide as she climbed all the way up, my eyes wary of the young girl when I was in the park. She fell, like I had suspected. I didn't think she was alone, but unfortunately, she was. So I helped her. Carefully piggy backing her on my back, her arms wrapped around my neck. I brought her home as she sniffled the address in my ear, clutching my shirt as if I would dare to make her fall. I met Hayden for the first time, a striking image of his little sister with angular features, ocean-blue eyes and dark hair.

He had turned pale watching his little sister's knee bleeding, gently applying the *Hello Kitty* bandage while I offered her a candy to distract her.

I had watched her grow, seen her get her braces and get them removed, bought her favorite doughnuts when she got her first periods, heard her talk about her awkward first kiss under the bleachers because she was too scared to talk about it with Hayden and get embarrassed by her friends. I had picked her up from her prom after party, gave her my hoodie and bought her ice cream at three in the morning. I had hugged her goodbye when I left with her brother for his deployment and my work, hoping she would take care of herself.

I cared about Ivy. My little petal. That was why I was going to do terrible things to the person, to the shit, who made her cry.

It was also why it was unfortunate that my third thought was widely different from the first two. I hated being myself when I thought of her… *differently*. I was truly a sadist to get turned on by her red, watery eyes. All I could think about was wrapping my fist around her hair and seeing her sky eyes gleam with tears of pain and pleasure, hazy with lust, but trusting me to take care of her and her needs. Being on her knees with my hands on her face and fucking those pouty lips—

"Fuck," I breathed, swallowing the lump in my throat and glaring at the semi in my sweatpants. I had to stop thinking about her.

Which won't happen when she is under the same roof, taking a shower, all wet and naked—

I closed my eyes and thought about all the ways I helped my patients with their anxiety. I took four deep breaths. After clearing my heads of all the filthy thoughts, I made a list of why I should never think about the said filthy thoughts.

1. She is Ivy Knight.

2. She is Hayden Knight's little sister, my best friend's sister, and he would dump me in the Arctic Ocean if he ever knew about these thoughts.

3. She is young. Eleven years younger than I am.

4. She probably thinks of me as her elder brother.

5. Did I mention she is related to Hayden Knight? The person who can and will murder me if I ever thought about touching her inappropriately.

Yes, that list was good and it should help remind me every time my blood rushes to the south. But it was the fourth point that truly scared me. I knew I had been overly protective of her when we were young—I still was, but I never meant it in a brotherly way. No, I just didn't want her to get hurt. I wanted to care for her. But not the way a sibling does.

As if he knew I was thinking about him, Hayden called me. I picked up after one more ring, hearing him say, "Hey, asshole. Did you miss your favorite person?"

"Hello to you too, darling," I said, stirring the red sauce, hating myself for the small twitch on my lips. Hayden Knight was a pain in the ass, but he was my close friend. We had been mistaken for brothers, but it was clear from one closer look that our eyes didn't match and he was more charming with talking our way out of a situation. "Why on earth would I miss you out of everyone? In fact, I'm glad your Azmian princess whisked you off of San Diego and keeps you locked in her palace."

I heard a shuffle and a soft feminine voice. "Aw, Aiden! I knew you secretly liked me underneath all that 'I hate everyone, people are stupid' guise!" I shook my head hearing Zara

Knight Latif, the Princess of Azmia, and the fiancée of my best friend, try to mimic my voice.

"Why are you out of bed?" Hayden asked her and for a moment, all I heard was poor reception and clothes shuffling. "You should've called me, I would have—"

Zara didn't let him finish. "Aiden, tell your friend that I won't fall the second he looks away."

"You would've landed on your bump if you had looked where you walked."

"I would love to see where I'm walking, but I can't see my feet, you ass."

"Then hold my hand, I'm here for—"

I cleared my throat, watching the steam rolling off of the pasta in the pan. "As much as I'd love to hear you both bicker, I have something to tell you, Hayden."

"I'll leave you boys to it."

Hayden yelled when she walked away, "Please have a guard with you!"

My heart felt heavy hearing them bicker lovingly. Hayden had saved the life of Princess of Azmia, promised her safety, care and love for their engagement and even trying his best to be a good father for his soon-to-be-child and a good husband when they get married.

Hayden, the man who had fucked his way through half of the San Diego's single women, was now expecting a child and marrying the woman he met once and pinned on her for two years, so much so that he never once flirted with anyone. It was unusual for him to stay celibate for so long. He was utterly whipped.

"All well?"

I heard him sigh. "Pregnancy is a hard thing."

I chuckled, "You don't say."

"I'm serious. All her mood swings affect me and I don't

know what it is, but I can't stand anyone looking at her when she is pregnant with my child—"

"You've been reading too many fantasy romances—"

I could hear him grin when he replied, "Maybe. Zayed asked me to try one and I'm stuck now." Zayed was the Sheikh of Azmia and his good friend. "Anyway, how was the date?"

"Date?" I pinched the bridge of my nose and remembered how last night went when I had arrived in San Diego. The expensive wine, dessert and a hotel room. "It went well, I suppose. A one-night stand. But it doesn't matter, I need to tell you something—"

"Was it that bad?" He asked from the other line, something shuffling.

"Hayden," I said, and he knew it was serious when I said his name. I turned off the stove and leaned back on the island. "I am at your house and you won't believe who showed up at the door."

"Addison in a trench coat?"

Hearing the name of my ex made me lose my appetite. If she had appeared like that, which she would never have, I would have locked the door on her face.

"She would never do that." I sighed. "It was your sister with a suitcase. She was crying. I believe something happened with her bo—"

"Is she okay? Should I come back—wait, let me check the ticket—"

"Hayden, she is twenty-one. She can take care of herself... and I am here, too."

He didn't reply for a few moments. I held my breath.

"Yes, I trust you, of course," he sighed. I clenched my hand in a fist. Another reason for hating myself to even have a hint of attraction towards his sister. "I will see if I can come back, but I need you to talk to her, Aiden."

"Of course, I will talk with her—"

"No, Aiden," he paused. "I meant, as a therapist."

"What do you mean?"

"You know how it was when mom left. When *we* left. She hasn't been herself since she went to university. With Zara here, she lost her close best friend, and I have been trying to talk to her, see her, but I need your help. I don't want her to feel insecure. If you can, I want you to talk to her, give her a few therapy sessions. If not you, someone else."

I knew what he meant. Her mom had divorced her father and left. Her father couldn't cope with the sudden loss and ignored both of his children. Hayden was a senior in high school, but Ivy was barely six years old and had no one. They both had tried to bond with each other, but she never had a parent figure in her life and it may have affected her. Not to mention the insecure part. She was beautiful and curvy, but being a therapist for so long, I knew that even the most beautiful person on the earth viewed themselves differently in front of the mirror.

"I will take care of her." I clenched the phone in my hand and said, "You don't have to worry about it."

"Thank you. I will call Ivy tonight. See you soon."

"You too," I replied, ending the call. Staring at the cooked spaghetti, I let out a sigh, raking my hand through my hair.

His phone call was a living reminder that I should not think about—

"Did you cook this for me?"

Ivy was wearing the same fucking hoodie that I had given her on her prom night. *It's not going to lick itself*, it said in bold white letters. I wondered if she knew what it meant. Hayden would punch me if he knew I had given *that* hoodie to his sister. His little sister, who was wearing just the hoodie, the hem reaching her creamy plush thighs.

I licked my lips, turning my back to her, and tried hard

not to wonder if she was wearing anything underneath that hoodie.

"You should eat it before it gets cold," I said, serving the hot spaghetti in red sauce. I kept the plate on the table and pulled out a chair for her, motioning her to sit, my nose filling with the sweet floral scent of her shampoo.

"Who were you talking to?" She asked, twirling the fork around the pasta and eating it. "Was it Hayden?"

I told her about his call, about Zara and how he would call her soon and that she should stay in the house for a while until the university classes start again and she has to go back to dorm. After asking about her business school, I brought up the main point I wanted to discuss with her.

"Why do you have that thinking-face on?" Ivy asked with a small smile, keeping the plates in the dishwasher.

I managed to keep my eyes on her face and not her bare thighs. Or how amazing her chest looked in the hoodie. *She's definitely not wearing a bra.* "Thinking face?"

She nodded, her finger hovering over my eyes and mouth. I ignored the urge to pull her closer, hold her wrist and check for myself if she was wearing anything underneath that damn hoodie.

"Your eyebrows are pinched together and you have that dark gleam in your eyes whenever you are thinking," Ivy said, her voice light. Her blue eyes dropped to my mouth. After three seconds, she looked away, licking her lips.

I didn't think it would be wise to tell her that that was my I-want-to-take-you-over-my-lap-and-check-if-you-are-naked-underneath-my-hoodie-and-spank-you-like-the-naughty-brat-you-are look.

"I agreed with your brother that I will have a few sessions with you," I said, holding her wrist and lowering it from my face so I could meet her eyes. Her pulse was beating wildly underneath my thumb.

"Sessions?" She breathed.

Naughty. Fucking. Girl.

The corner of my mouth curled. "Not those kinds of sessions, you naughty little Petal," I crooned, slowly rubbing the pad of my thumb over her pulse. "Therapy sessions."

"I wasn't thinking anything." Her cheeks turned the loveliest shade of pink. "Therapy sessions? What? You will be my therapist then?"

"Yes, Petal." I let go off of her wrist and stood up, easily towering over her as she craned her head to look at me. "I will be your therapist and you will be my patient." I said the words that I'd never say in front of her like a porn star about to bend her over the dining table.

And like the beginning of any porno, she stuttered, wide doe-eyes blinking up at me.

"But I am…" she trailed off.

I raised my brow and continued, "If you don't want to sit in the same room with me after tomorrow's session, Hayden or I won't bother you again, Ivy. Give me one day, one hour."

Her slender throat bobbed as she blinked up at me. I held the reins of my dirty thoughts and watched the way her face softened, agreeing with me like I knew she would.

"Okay, I will have a session with you," she whispered.

I hid my smile.

Good. Fucking. Girl.

3
USE YOUR TONGUE

IVY

"I'm telling you nothing happened, Ivy," Jason drawled in the cell phone while I heard a small giggle in the background.

My heart ached, not for him, but for me, who fell for his charms. "You both were naked and kissing on our bed. Doing more than just kissing and you're telling me nothing happened?"

My hands clenched into fist, hoping my tone stays even and doesn't waver. It was hard for me to speak up during conflicts, but over the past two weeks of therapy sessions with Aiden or as I liked to call him—Doctor Aiden, during the sessions, has helped a lot.

"You're mistaking—"

"I need to go. Stop calling me."

I heard him scoffed when I was about to end the call. "Whatever, you are fat anyway."

I bit my bottom lip and forced the tears back. I was already late for the session and didn't want to waste my time overthinking about what my ex said in the end.

"Sorry, I had a call," I said, closing the door behind me. I looked at the comfortable pale blue couch and sat in the middle without meeting his eyes like I always do.Because I knew he will know something had happened, and he'd ask me to talk about it—about him and I couldn't.

His clinic was not at all like I had imagined. It was minimalist and cozy, with his certificates and various awards lined on the wall behind his desk. The bookshelf comprised a few books and antiques and craft pieces his patients had gifted him. There was a coffee table between the two couches that faced each other that always had sweets, savory snacks, tissues, and a candle.

His obsidian dark eyes kept looking at me through the thin framed glasses that should not make him more attractive than he already was. But they did. It was unfair how deliciously hot he looked in them. It made me want to lean closer and take away his glasses to see what he would do. His hair was sleeked back, his stubble neatly trimmed over his sharp jaw. A crisp gray shirt stretched over his broad shoulders with sleeves rolled over his forearms and the veins on his arms shifted ever so slightly when he wrote something in his diary.

I licked my dry lips.

The cursed frame glasses perched on his strong pointed nose, his soft lips in a thin line, made him look like the main cast of a high school porn video. Worse thing was that I could imagine him as a stern hot teacher, punishing student over his lap—

My mental pornography starring the man across from me came to a halt when he said, "Whose call was it?"

Smoothing my hand over my flowy white skirt, I lied. "Oh, i-it was nothing important."

Aiden's eyes narrowed, my eyes fixed on his hands. His long fingers closed the diary as he stood up from the chair behind his desk and strode towards the small couch across me. His movements were graceful, confident.

If I tried walking without looking at the floor like that, I would get my shoe stuck on the rug and trip.

"You are still a terrible liar, little Petal," he said in his smooth voice, his legs widening when he sat down. A spectacular image of a composed gentleman, a notepad on his thigh with a pen.

I was a terrible person to be jealous of that notepad.

"I am not little anymore," I argued weakly.

I felt little and small compared to *him*. It wasn't because he was tall or more than a decade older than me. It was something else entirely that gave me the shivers and made my heart rate increase. The way he presented himself and the surrounding air, always charged with something that made me intimidated by him ever since I met him.

"I am twenty-one now." I said, raising my chin a little. "I am a big girl."

Aiden smiled, as if he knew how little I felt around him. That my age had nothing to do with it. He shifted, crossing his leg, his shiny black shoes gleaming in the light of his office.

I swallowed the lump in my throat when he peered over his glasses and said, "We will talk about that call at the end. Tell me about your day."

I started, much more relaxed, since the first day. I was frozen and tensed at the start of the first session, but Aiden was wonderful. Listening to me, his expression was impassive yet soothed me to say it all out loud. About how I truly felt when mom left, the emotional detachment from my father, how lonely I felt when Hayden had to leave for his studies and then work. How I was bullied and awkward when it came to making new friends. How different Jason had made me feel.

The corners of his mouth twitched whenever I mentioned Jason, my ex-boyfriend, as if he had some sort of dislike towards him. I knew that expression well, because he made that same face whenever we had seafood. *He hates seafood. Does that mean he hates Jason too?*

"And how do you feel now?" He asked, removing his glasses and pinning his eyes on me.

"Better." I blinked, not knowing how to put it into words. So, I stuck with, "Much better than how I was when I broke up with Jason."

His lips twitched again. "Hm, have you been doing your assignments?"

Assignments comprised little daily puzzles and affirmations which he had asked me to do every day. Especially after ending each session, to know my emotions better. I cherished his secret smiles when he would find me doing them at the kitchen island after our dinner. I secretly did it for his smile. Wanting to please him. I enjoyed doing them, reflecting on myself and figuring out what I wanted with introspection little by little each day. It gave me more clarity and assurance and acceptance of who I was as a person. I also enjoyed pleasing Aiden, making him smile because of me.

Although the hardest were the affirmations regarding my body and self-image. It was difficult, but now I could do them without crying and thinking I don't deserve to be called beautiful. I was improving and feeling better because of the handsome man sitting across from me. And if I said that to him, he'd tell me that it was all me and he just helped me show the way.

"Yes, sir," I said, beaming proudly at him.

My heart stuttered when his eyes flickered to me, a dark gleam in them after hearing my reply. I scrambled my thoughts, wondering if I had said anything wrong. I didn't want to disappoint him by saying something wrong—but then again, he knew all the good and ugly parts about me in just a few days.

"Good," he replied, clearing his throat. "Before we end this session, I want to ask you about that phone call."

The tone of his voice had changed. He wasn't being a professional therapist anymore, he was being my brother's best-friend. A concerned brother's best-friend.

I hated it. Because I knew, despite of how infatuated I was with him, all he could see was his friend's silly little sister. Never anything else.

Clenching my hands, I said, "It's none of your business, Aiden."

He didn't reply for a few moments. I held my breath, counting each second. I swear I could feel the pressure increasing in the room, pressing down on my skin in the light airy room that resembled peace and safety. But now it felt heavy... and scary. Scary in a good way. It was anticipation burning through my veins, my heartbeat increasing with each second.

"Is that any way to use your mouth in front of me, Petal?" Aiden asked, his voice rumbling through my bones, caressing the innermost parts of me as he leaned back. Arrogance and something terribly arousing rolled off of him. It curled around my body, sizzling me and making me want to do terrible things for him—

I should have taken my backpack and rushed out of the room if I was smarter. But I wasn't. I wanted to see with my own eyes how he would react.

Tilting my head, I heard myself say, "Do you want to see how I use my mouth, Doctor Aiden?"

His eyes turned darker, almost onyx, despite how bright the room was. He opened his mouth to reply, but my phone rang with a shrill ringtone. It was one of the rules to keep it silenced, but I had forgotten today after the chat with Jason before the session.

"It's him, isn't it?" He asked as I checked the caller ID.

"I am sorry, but I have to take th—"

I gaped when he took my phone from my hands and accepted it, pressing it against his ear. My eyes betrayed me for a moment, falling over his muscular, strong thighs, the way his pants fitted him perfectly. Especially that ass—

Focus Ivy!

I am.

Not *on his ass.*

"No, you fucking prick. Have some decency to accept you cheated on her," Aiden snapped.

My eyes widened hearing Jason's voice on the other side of the call, a vein popping on Aiden's neck. He seemed furious. I had never seen him that way before.

His eyes flickered to me for a moment. With his jaw clenched, he answered, "Fortunately, I am not like you, so I won't answer that vulgar question of yours. Instead, you should spend those brain cells to reflect on your life choices that made you end up here. Calling the sweetest girl you had the honor to date, after cheating on her and begging her to take you back. Do yourself a favor and don't dare to call her again."

I was still gaping when he ended the call, presumably blocking his number and handing me the phone. I quickly closed my mouth when Aiden's face appeared in front of mine, with only an inch separating us. I could smell his cologne, the sharp musky male scent making me want to lean closer and press my nose against the collar of his neck.

His eyes dropped to my lips when I licked them. I held in my breath when his warm finger tucked a piece of hair behind my ear. "Despite everything stopping me, little Petal, I would love to see how you use this pretty mouth of yours," he whispered, my belly tightening.

I clenched my thighs when he stood up and took a step back, his piercing dark eyes pinned on me. "Before you leave, take the diary from my desk and write about your emotions and feelings."

It took me a few moments to gather my thoughts and reply, "You want me to journal?"

"Yes, Ivy. Journal your daily thoughts. As soon as you wake up and before you go to sleep." He sat down on his chair and opened the drawer, giving me a leather-bound black diary. I started from his face and the diary when he clasped his hands and leaned on the desk. "Can you do that for me?"

Yes, Doctor Aiden. *Should I kneel and suck your cock, too?*

With a flushed face, I scolded my mind for going into the gutter at such an inappropriate time. I took the diary and looked through the blank pages.

"Only my emotions?" I asked.

"Whatever makes you happy, sad, angry, disappointed, anything. I want you to write about what makes you feel. And bring this with you next week, okay?"

I could do that. I could write about my emotions every day and night. I nodded, keeping the diary in my bag.

Aiden said with a much deeper and commanding voice, "I asked you something, Petal. Use your tongue and answer me."

I blinked at him, at the sudden change in the air. "I-I..." I forgot what I was going to say. "Y-yes, Doctor Aiden. Of course, yes, *um*. I will bring the diary with me during the next session." I stammered, and by the twitch in his sharp jaw covered in little stubble, I knew he had noticed my nervousness.

"Good girl."

4
I AM ALWAYS HERE IF YOU GET SCARED

IVY

I had practically sprinted out of his office, almost making fun of myself, when I tripped on my shoes. Thankfully, I didn't fall flat on my face. Knowing him, he would be busy with his work, so I reached home and tried to ignore the burning sensation between my legs and make us some dinner.

For two weeks, we had fallen into a routine. He would wake up early to go to the gym and make us breakfast. By the time I got ready and had my breakfast, he would be back home, showered and ready in his crisp shirt and silk pants, making a small lunch for both of us. I would cook the dinner and we both would have it together, sometimes calling Hayden and Zara. It almost felt like how it was before.

My stomach tightened with nerves when I heard the front door open. Even before he stepped into the kitchen, I knew it was Aiden, the intense air thickening with sexual tension when he greeted me.

"You're early," I said.

He tilted his head. "I didn't have any more appointments. Do you need my help?"

I shook my head. "You can go freshen up. We can have an early dinner."

Aiden nodded, unbuttoning the top few buttons of his shirt. I swallowed, my eyes greedily taking in the tanned, muscled skin. "We should watch a movie together. It's been a while since we had any movie nights."

* * *

MOVIE NIGHT WAS A TERRIBLE IDEA.

"Are you sure you are not scared?" Aiden asked, his voice low when the creaking paranormal sound continued from the flat screen of the television.

I had my eyes squeezed shut. "I'm not scared," I lied pathetically, my voice nothing but a mere whimper.

I heard him sigh somewhere beside me on the couch and felt the warm blanket around my shoulders. I made a small sound at the back of my throat when he pulled me flush to his side, his arm holding me close.

"Now you can hide your face whenever you want, little Petal," he crooned, his lips pecking my hair.

"Stop babying me," I said, my eyes fixed on his side profile, the sharp jaw, his stubble, long lashes creating shadows on his cheeks.

"Then stop being a baby." He turned towards me, my heart rate increasing. "It's just a horror film. No one is going to haunt you."

I didn't believe him.

Aiden shifted, and I held my breath. Not because of the horror film, but because of how warm his body felt against my side. It was perfect, the easy, comfortable way we fitted together. I clenched my thighs, ignoring his strong, hot body.

"Do you want to watch something else?" He asked, his voice smooth, his hand gently running thorough my hair. I wanted to press myself against him and have his fingers run through my scalp.

"You wanted to watch this movie," I argued.

"Because you chose this," he said. "I asked you before to choose a rom-com, but you assured me you will watch this."

Aiden was right. I picked the horror film because I wanted to show him that I was not little anymore and... I wanted to please him. I knew he enjoyed watching horror films with Hayden, how they would laugh at certain scenes and mockingly scare each other. I never stayed up to watch paranormal stuff with them. It always terrified me.

I looked between him and the television. Squealing at the horrifying jump scare, I pressed my cheek against Aiden's chest and squeezed my eyes shut. His arm tightened around me and I heard the film music stop.

"Come on, Petal, you can open your eyes now," he said softly. "It's gone now."

"Promise?"

"Yes, I promise."

Trusting him, I opened my eyes and noticed the television was turned off. The living room was dark, a dim yellow lamp lit in the room's corner. I shifted towards Aiden and realized I had jumped on his lap during the scary scene.

His eyes were pinned on my face, his hand rubbing my back soothingly, allowing me to stay on his lap. I bit my lip, knowing he could feel that I wasn't wearing any bra underneath the worn-out tee shirt of my brother.

Shit, my brother. I had forgotten that Aiden was my brother's best friend first. He saw me as his little sister.

"I'm sorry," I said, trying to stand up from his thighs, but he stopped me.

"Shh, Ivy," he said, his warm breath brushing my cheeks. "*Stay*. I know you are scared. Your heart beat has increased."

It increased because I was on the lap of my childhood crush.

I didn't complain as the side of my body relaxed on his strong chest. I could hear his steady heartbeat, smell the musky scent of his cologne. I wish I could press my nose against his tee shirt and inhale his male scent. Closing my eyes, I made myself comfortable on his lap.

After a few moments, I don't know when I woke up in my bed. The blanket covered me and the fairy lights were on. The door of my bedroom was kept ajar. Aiden must have—

The curtain of the window flew in the dark, and my heart pounded in my ears. *Nope.* Not sleeping alone tonight. I took my pillow and tiptoed out of my room. In my sleepy haze, I knocked on the door. He opened it after a few seconds, raising his brow at me.

"I can't sleep alone," I said sheepishly, looking down at the floor. "I got scared."

I was surprised to feel his hand on my arm tugging me inside. "I know, Petal." He brought me to his bed and said, "I am always here if you get scared."

The sheets of his bed were dark gray as I laid down on one side, nuzzling deeper in the pillows that smelled like him. I felt the slightest brush of his knuckles on my cheeks as he whispered goodnight and switched off the lights. I didn't get scared the entire night, sleeping like a baby because I knew Aiden was sleeping a few inches away from me. Protecting me.

* * *

I WOKE UP SQUIRMING. Wet arousal pooling in my underwear as I looked around the empty bedroom of Aiden. It was seven in the morning and I knew he would be at the gym.

Lying back on his bed, the smell of pine and his cologne wafted in my nose. I played the images of the wet dream in my head, his large hands stroking my body, ordering me to finish my assignments on time and showing him how I used my mouth on his hard length as he praised and degraded me.

Biting my lip, I slipped my hand underneath my pajama shorts, feeling the damp arousal on my underwear before moving it to the side and pressing my finger against the aching clit. A small moan slipped out of me. His name was on my lips as I whimpered, pushing two fingers inside me and twisting my pebbled nipples with my other hand.

"Aiden," I whispered breathily. "Please..."

I groaned, the sound of my fingers dipping inside me turning me on. Wishing they were his fingers, thicker and longer. His other hand pinning down my thigh, forcing me to stay still while he bruised my pussy with his hands and mouth, overstimulating me and edging me. I imagined his commanding voice whispering in my ear to spread my legs wider and not to come until he said so.

"Please fuck me," I whimpered, squeezing my eyes shut and arching my back. The cool sheets were a reminder that I was in his bedroom, his scent overpowering me.

I bit down on a pillow to muffle my moans when I orgasmed. I breathed loudly, gaping at the ceiling as my fingers drenched with my cum, my core throbbing and sensitive, my nipples red.

That was one of the most intense orgasms I have ever had. And *that* fast.

Shaking my head, I sat up on the bed, blushing at the sight of my spread legs in front of the mirror. My face flushed. My hair was a tousled mess. I wondered how it would feel to have his large warm hands fondling my sensitive breasts, his fingers tweaking my nipples until I moaned with pain and pleasure.

I am a mess.

I made the bed, making sure that my arousal hadn't left any stain on the bedsheets. I straightened my tee shirt, patted my hair, and opened the door.

My heart dropped in my stomach.

"Aiden…"

5
I HATE LIARS

AIDEN

I was expecting to see Ivy sleeping between my pillows and blankets, her pouty lips parted, looking like a sweet angel.

What I was not expecting was her soft voice, whispering my name over and over again with a gasp between them. As soon as I walked upstairs, ready to wake her up after my early workout in the gym, I heard her moans.

Her sinful whimpers drew me closer to the unlocked door, my eyes squeezing shut.

"Aiden," I heard her breathy voice. *"Please…"*

My skin tightened, and blood rushed down to my crotch. I clenched my jaw, controlling myself with pure will when my dick pressed against the boxers, urging me to use my hand. Or barge inside and order her to beg more. Hear her little whines of desperation. Tell me what she wanted.

My naughty little Petal.

I heard the wet sounds of her cunt, soaked with her arousal. My breathing turned harsh, and I wanted nothing more than to wrap my hand around her throat and use my hands on her. Plunge my fingers inside her dripping sex, choking her until she begged me to come.

But I wouldn't allow her to come until she begged prettily, used her pouty lips on me. *Fuck*. What I wouldn't do to feel her warm mouth around me, her blue eyes tearing up when I feed her my cock.

"Please fuck me."

I exhaled sharply, hearing her muffled moans. I knew she came, climaxed in my bed with her fingers covered in her cum, trying so badly to stifle her whimpers. I counted to ten, controlling my breathing and forcing my boner down.

If I acted on my urges, I would take her pretty ass over my lap, spank her and have her throat fucked before she would beg me to fuck her. I wouldn't be gentle, I would be rough. I didn't want that for Ivy. If it had been someone else moaning my name, I would have fucked them by now and told them to leave. But I couldn't do that to Ivy.

Never with my Petal. She deserved more.

I would need a lot of hours to worship her body, memorize the curves of her skin on my tongue and lips before edging and denying her orgasms. Until she was nothing but a desperate, wet, needy Petal. Then I would slide inside her, holding her neck to see her eyes pinned on me, reminding her I was making her feel all the pain and pleasure.

Hearing the soft rustling sound of my bedsheets, I straightened up. A moment later, the door opened.

I gazed at the wide blue eyes of Ivy. Wearing nothing but a long tee shirt that reached her thighs. I wanted to turn her around and pin her to the wall. Yank that tee shirt over her ass and give it a good spanking before checking how wet she was from her orgasm.

Would she enjoy my hands on her body? Manhandling her, holding her, ordering her to stay still? Would that make her pretty pussy wet?

"Aiden..."

"Little Petal," I drawled, my eyes dipping to her chest. Her nipples pebbled underneath my scorching stare. *Naughty mixen.* I raised my eyes and asked, innocence lacing my voice, "Did you just wake up?"

Her cheeks flushed, and she tried to cover her breasts with her hair, crossing her arms. "I did," she lied, faking a yawn. "I might sleep in today before our session."

I let her walk past me, the scent of feminine arousal and the musky scent of sex clinging to her. I let her because I didn't trust myself to be gentle with her when she had just lied to me.

"Ivy."

She stopped, turning towards me with wide eyes, knowing I rarely called her by her first name. "One thing you should remember is that I hate liars."

Her body shuddered, her eyes tracking over my clothes, my skin, covered in a thin sheet of sweat from strength training.

She licked her lips. "You do?"

"Yes. I prefer bitter truth than sweet lies, Ivy. Even if the truth seems daunting."

She knew that I knew.

"What do you do when you catch a liar?" She asked, her eyes dancing with curiosity. It was no doubt that she found it thrilling. Wanting to know what I would do next.

"I make them confess the truth." Leaning closer to her face, I whispered in her ear, "And if a liar is as pretty as you, I punish them."

I pulled away, watching her breasts heave, a red flush creeping up her neck. "P-punish them?"

I hummed.

"How?"

Smiling darkly, I tapped her nose. "Let's hope you won't have to find that out, Petal." I turned, walking into my room. Pausing, I said, "Don't be late like yesterday. I don't like tardiness."

Before I could close the door, Ivy said, "Or what? You'll punish me too?"

I gazed at her through my lashes, her curvy frame and the teasing smile on her lips. She didn't know how dark my desires went, how she fueled them since the day I had the urge to protect her.

Keep her safe and ruin her for me.

"I will if I have to, little Petal."

* * *

"And this is the third guest room," the pretty redhead waved her arm around the empty room as I glanced around the walls. I walked past her, towards the window that was directly against the house across from the one I was standing in. And a kid, no—a girl was playing with her gaming controller as a man joined her in the living room, ruffling her hair and picking up another controller.

I clenched my jaw and glared at the redhead, my real estate agent. Her eyes turned wide, seeing my face, and she looked away.

"You didn't tell me this house had neighbors."

"W-well, Mister Aiden, this is the only house that fits all your needs from two garages to more rooms and security. I'm sure you can overlook neighbors living in such a cozy home. And those are the Millers, I can introduce to them when we—"

"No need." I left the room. I wasn't here to make neighbors, just to see another house from the few that had disappointed me. Miss Poppy, the real estate agent, was right. The house suited me perfectly, with tall ceilings, beige walls, a fireplace, and more rooms than I'd ever need.

It would have been perfect for a family if—

I wasn't going there. Addison had shown her true colors, and that was it. I was moving on. I had already moved from Denver and the house could be another step.

"Do you want to check the pool?"

"No, thank you." I tilted my head and said, "Where can I sign the papers?"

Forty-five minutes later, I walked out of the agency building with a set of keys in my pocket and a bottle of Champagne gifted from a very flushed Poppy. I hope her boss paid her well. She was sweet and professional.

Checking my watch, I sat in the driver's seat in my car. Thirty minutes to start my session with Ivy. She didn't know I was looking at houses. I could take her to dinner—*no, that's too romantic*. I could order Chinese takeout to celebrate and we could watch another movie together.

6
WHY ARE YOU LYING TO ME?

IVY

"No, tell me, did he do that thing with his tongue?"

I giggled, seeing her scrunched face, and shook my head. Her English accent was stronger as she lived in Azmia, in the Golden Palace, and it made me happy seeing her glowing, warm face.

"Why are you laughing? I'm serious, I want to know."

"No, Zara, he didn't... he didn't do anything with his tongue."

She said nothing for a moment, straightening her phone, the background of one of the gardens in the palace as she walked slowly, guards following her as she finally said,

"What an asshole."

I chuckled, playing with the hem of my dress. "I still can't believe you are a Princess."

Her smile softened, her short dark hair framing her elfin face with sharp cheekbones and hazel eyes that glinted in the sunlight. "I apologize for not telling you sooner about... everything, Ivy."

I knew. She had apologized and accepted my brother's

proposal, the same man whom she was pining over for years until she stumbled into him in our house.

"It's okay, Zara. I forgave you a long time ago."

"Did you tell Hayden about him?" Her expression grew dark.

I sighed and rolled on my back on the bed, looking at the ceiling. "If I tell him that Jason cheated on me with my roommate, he would get mad. Very mad."

"Furious." She noted.

"Mhm, and I don't care about it anymore," I lied. Of course, I cared about it. My first ever boyfriend cheated on me. With my friend and my roommate. "I just want to move on, focus on my studies, you know."

"And Aiden."

My cheeks turned red, thinking about him. She knew about my little crush on him, and she hadn't stopped convincing me to confess to him and know if he likes me or not.

But I'm too scared to do it.

"You should ask him before you end up getting hurt, Ivy."

I eyed the closed door of my room. "Maybe you are right, Zara. But you didn't see how he looked at me this morning. He looked… hungry."

Like he wanted to eat me.

Her soft laugh made me smile. "Did he look hungry for breakfast, or you?"

I didn't reply, my cheeks warming.

"You have it bad for him, sweetheart."

"I know. He is very kind and generous with me. I love talking to him more than Hayden because he doesn't treat me like a little sister… even though he might think of me that way."

"Oh, Ivy. You should talk to him about your feelings. Tell him you don't see him as your elder brother," she said as she walked from the garden into the Palace, nodding at the maids and guards who bowed at her.

"Please tell me you blocked Jason. If he does anything, I can ask my brothers to—"

"Aiden did."

"Explain."

I blushed thinking about how hot he looked when he swore at him, the vein on his neck looking very inviting. "Jason called me during the therapy session and Aiden picked it up. He threatened him and told him not to call me again, blocking his number."

"That's good."

"So, he is now sending me emails and apologizing for having sex with Amanda."

"He is a dick. Block him everywhere."

"I will—*oh shit*, Zara, I am so sorry but I have to go," I panicked, checking the time, running around my room to shove things into my handbag. Chapstick, sunscreen, house keys and the journal. I didn't have the time to take out the ruffled papers I had placed inside it and shoved everything inside my bag. "I am going to be late for the therapy session."

"I love you, bye!"

I sent her a flying kiss as she ended the call. If I drive fast enough and the traffic gods are with me, I can make it in time. Even five minutes early.

* * *

I DIDN'T MAKE it in time.

"I am so sorry, Aiden, the traffic was so bad," I heaved, taking support of my knees to control my breathing. So much for dressing up in a cute dress, applying light makeup and curling my hair in waves for the session. I wiped down the sweat from my forehead and straightened up, daring to peek at him.

Aiden looked like he always did. His face was stern, without any emotions. His eyes traveled down my body, and I held in my shiver when they raked over my bare legs.

He made a dramatic point of checking his wristwatch that cost more than the car I drove and hummed. "We will talk about your tardiness after the session. *Sit.*"

I quickly sat down and drank some water, the cool air of the air conditioner breezing through my skin. The session started, and we made usual talk about my day, what happened that week or if anything exciting happened that I wanted to share with him. There was one moment where I was emotionally overwhelmed when he asked me a couple of questions about my childhood and my ignorant father. But he looked proud of me when I answered them patiently and quietly, without tears pooling in my eyes like all the sessions before.

He had told me it would take time to go through my childhood and remember certain instances, but he would be there for me and we could always talk about something else.

"You seem quite happy today, Ivy," Aiden said, noting something. I ignored the disappointment when he didn't call me by my nickname. I liked my name, but he always called me Petal.

I twisted my fingers on my lap, the flimsy material of the dress brushing over my thighs. "Yes, I am happy. I am enjoying the vacation, reading books and even called my friend."

Aiden looked up. "Which friend?"

I grinned. "Zara, Hayden's fiancée. She showed me the Palace gardens and told me I can visit Azmia anytime."

"I am glad you have a friend you can rely on, Petal," he said with a smile.

I crossed my leg and tried not to think about that same smile between my legs, teasing me with his tongue, teeth, and lips.

He asked me about my other friends.

"I haven't talked to Noah for a while, but we usually DM each other on Instagram."

His pen halted, and he looked at me, tilting his head. *"Noah?"*

"Yes, he is a really good friend of mine. Very sweet and charming. He always buys me iced coffee when we study together in the library during finals."

"Hm." Aiden didn't ask anything more about him and questioned, "And you lived in a dorm, right? What about your roommate?"

My smile dropped, and I looked at the coffee table between us. Somewhere inside his office, a paper rustled and the sound of swallowing the lump in my throat reminded me of my friend having sex with my boyfriend—ex-boyfriend— in my room.

"Ivy?"

I blinked at Aiden and shook my head. "It's n-nothing."

"Tell me." He said, "Take a deep breath and tell me about your roommate."

So I told him about Amanda. Scrunching my hands into fists as I recalled the events of that day. Going to my dorms late at night after studying for hours in library and thinking Amanda had another guy over like all the other times, but the shoes belonged to Jason. I had gifted them to him for our three-month anniversary and walking into my room to see both of them embracing each other, moaning each other's names. Jason had never touched me like that. *Never.*

"He cheated on you. With your roommate. Your friend." Aiden's expression was blank, but I knew he was angry. His dark gray eyes had turned almost onyx, and it made me feel warm.

"Yes." I shrugged. "I left them and came back in the morning to pack my bags and come home to be with my brother. You know the rest."

There was silence in the office. I had gotten used to it.

"And how did that made you feel, Ivy? Seeing your boyfriend—"

"Ex-boyfriend." I corrected him.

"Yes. Seeing your ex-boyfriend with a person who you thought was your friend?"

"It hurt." I sniffled and blinked my eyes. *I won't cry. I won't cry. I won't cry.* "It still hurts. I thought he liked me for me even though I'm fat. I thought he even loved me, but you don't hurt the person you love. Not like that."

"Do you want to talk more about it?" He asked softly, knowing well that if we delved into it, I would cry.

I shook my head and pursed my lips.

"Okay, tell me about your journaling."

We talked more about the days where I would write two-three pages a day or days when I could barely write a paragraph. He listened to me and asked questions when I would stop talking, urging me to drink water and keep going.

"Do you mind if I see what you've written?" He asked, his dark eyes soft.

My muscles tensed as I met his obsidian eyes. They ran over my body and noticed how stiff I had become. My eyes lingered on his light blue shirt, stretching over his shoulders, the sleeves rolled up to his elbows, with a navy-colored tie. Maybe it was my imagination when I thought his eyes had stayed far too long on my chest and my legs. I shuffled in my seat and tucked the strand of my hair behind my ear.

Aiden's eyes flickered to my face, and he closed them for a moment, as if he was taking his time. He finally said, "You don't have to if you don't want me to read. I will understand and respect your privacy."

I licked my lips, trusting my instinct. "I-it's okay, I don't mind. You can read it."

I handed him the diary, frowning at the ruffled separate pages that I had shoved between them. He silently read the entry of my first day while I squirmed in my seat. I may or may not have drunk too much water, so I excused myself to the washroom.

When I came back, I could feel the change in the air. Aiden was sitting on the couch, but his posture was stiff. He barely addressed my presence when I sat down in my seat. I saw the diary was placed beside him and his jaw was clenched.

"Is everything okay?" I asked, my voice small.

He finally looked at me and the corner of his lips twitched. Leaning back on the couch, he said, "Yes, I suppose you could say that. I want to ask you something, Petal, and I want you to be honest about it."

Frowning, I nodded.

His eyes darkened, and he said in a stern voice, "Use your mouth."

"I—*um*, yes, Doctor Aiden."

I didn't know why I *felt* the need to address him seriously.

"What were you doing this morning?"

My eyes widened, my heart pounding in my ears. I glanced at the diary and it struck me. Those ruffled pages. *Shit, shit, shit*. After journaling every day for a week, I wrote my fantasies regarding Aiden on different torn pages. And how he loved my body, worshipped it. It made me feel better about myself, but I always tucked them back in the diary, reminding myself to pull them out before I brought it to the session. But I was in such a hurry that I had completely forgotten about them.

Did he read it? I hoped he didn't. I would rather eat raw broccoli than have him read all those pages.

Looking away from him, I lied and carelessly shrugged my shoulder. "I was meditating."

I mentally winced at my lie. He had tried coaching me to meditate, but I could never do it.

He is right. I am a terrible liar.

Aiden raised his eyebrows. "Is that so?"

I didn't like the tone of his voice. He seemed serious, and I prayed that the ground would swallow me up. He waited for my answer, crossing his arms over his chest. I got distracted by the way his biceps bulged.

He noticed me staring. I glanced down at my lap, twiddling my thumbs. "Y-yes, Doctor Aiden, I was meditating and I-I focused on my breath like you taught me—"

"Why are you lying to me, Ivy?"

My head snapped at him. *Ivy.* Not Petal.

I shook my head, "I-I am not lying."

Aiden tilted his head and my throat went dry when he said, "Then why did I hear your voice moaning my name when you orgasmed with your fingers inside your pussy?"

7
YOU FILTHY LITTLE GIRL

IVY

"W-what?"

Aiden placed the diary on the coffee table between us, including the ruffled pages all straightened out. I looked at the leather-bound diary and those pages with wide eyes.

He knows. He read it. He read how I fantasize about him.

"Look at me," he commanded, his voice deep.

I shook my head, closing my eyes and wanting to run away. I felt embarrassed. I didn't want him to look at me. I didn't want Aiden to know how I felt about him like that. Zara was right. Only if I had confessed my feelings before, none of this would have happened.

Aiden repeated himself, but it was a warning. "I said look at me, Petal."

I didn't move an inch, hoping, praying that it was all an embarrassing dream and I would wake up soon.

"I won't repeat, Petal." He said, his low voice making me shiver. "Look. At. Me."

Too scared and embarrassed to do something else, I

raised my eyes and saw the swirls of emotions in his onyx eyes.

With his jaw clenched, he nodded in front of him. "Come here."

I blabbered, "I am sorry, Aiden. I-I don't know what I was thinking. I *wasn't* thinking—"

He remained calm, but I knew he was angry that I had lied to him. "I didn't ask you to speak, did I? Come here, Ivy."

He said my name. Again.

Shit, I am in trouble.

I didn't move, my stomach clenching with nerves. The cold air felt sultry as it weighed over my prickling skin. The clock ticking on the wall behind me, assuring me of my impending doom.

"Now." He growled.

I gingerly stood up, swallowing the lump in my throat. I was about to walk towards him when Aiden said,

"*Crawl.*"

My jaw dropped. "What? I am not going to cr—"

"Yes, you will, Petal. Isn't that what you do in these fantasies of yours when you think about me dominating you, *hm?*" Aiden said, his commanding voice stirring something warm in my lower stomach. His intense gaze pierced my skin, urging me to bend to his will.

Well, he is right. But this is different.

I looked between him and the door to the hallway where his assistant sits at the cubicle desk.

"I asked Gary to leave early," he answered my unspoken question. *He knew this would happen. Ohmygod.* Clenching his jaw, he said, "Crawl to me, Ivy."

I shook my head, my fingers brushing over the hem of the dress and twisting it.

"If you won't crawl to me right now, I will discipline you." With his eyes on me, he continued, "Or you can leave this room right now, and I will assign you a new therapist, move to a new house, and never talk about this again."

My heart hurt at hearing the second option. I didn't want him to forget about whatever *this* was. I didn't want another therapist. I wanted him. *Only him.*

"Discipline me?"

"Do you want me to walk there and drag you here?"

Yes, please.

I shook out the mental image from my head and slowly lowered to my knees. I couldn't look him in the eye. It felt humiliating, yet my underwear was drenched with arousal. I pressed my palms on the soft white rug and squeezed my eyes shut when I got on all fours in front of Aiden. My brother's best friend. My crush.

"Open your eyes and look at me," he said in his low smoky voice, and it took everything in me not to tremble.

Taking a deep breath, I opened my eyes and looked at him. It should be illegal to be that handsome. His eyes were hooded and jaw sharp as he watched me slowly crawl towards him. My eyes averted to his loose tie, the tan chest peeking over the unbuttoned top button, down his perfectly fitted shirt to where I could see the outline of his bulge in his black slacks.

Oh shit.

With a flushed face, I tried to meet his eyes. They were lingering over my chest and my ass.

Was he getting turned on by this? Watching me on my hands and knees, crawling towards him?

Seeing that long bulge, it would seem so.

I was surprised when his hand ran through my hair when I reached him, my heartbeat getting faster at our proximity. I took a sharp breath when he gently tugged at my hair, lifting me until I was on my knees between his long legs. His throbbing erection tenting his slacks.

Licking my lips, I looked up at him and found a small smirk tugging at the corner of his lips. "Do you want to touch me, Petal?" With my wide eyes and flushed cheeks, I watched his magnificently long fingers lower the zipper of his pants and cup his boner through the boxers. "Do you want to touch my cock, *hm?*"

I nodded in a haze and flickered my eyes to his face. He was watching me intently. My face, my lips, the cleavage. I knew what he wanted, and there was no point in hiding my attraction towards him when he was getting turned on by watching me crawl towards him.

So, I leaned closer in a way that my plump breasts pressed against the couch, his eyes widening a little. His jaw clenched when I kept my hand on his, which was slowly sliding over his bulge, his skin warm.

My voice was a soft whisper when I said, "Please, let me touch you, Doctor Aiden." Taking a deep breath, I slid my other hand over his thigh, watching him and waiting for him to remove it, but he didn't. "I want to suck your cock."

His obsidian eyes curled with hunger and lust as he removed his hand and yanked my hair so that my flushed face was leaning over his crotch, my body bending over the couch with my hips in the air. I could smell him, his musky male scent, and squirmed, wanting that scent everywhere. All over me and inside me.

Aiden leaned closer, his lips pressing against the shell of my ear as he growled, "Suck me. Use that pretty little mouth on my cock and suck me off." He pressed closer, licking my ear. I shivered. "Until you swallow my cum."

He waited for me to push away from him, but I nodded and gently removed his boxers. Heat flushed my cheeks as I stared at his enlarged cock. Long with enough girth that I was sure I would feel a small pinch of pain if he fucked me in one hard thrust. I licked my lips at the thought and clenched my thighs, feeling more arousal seep out of me. I wanted to please him and swallow his cum like he wanted me to.

I can't believe my fantasy is coming alive.

Aiden's hand tightened on my scalp when I leaned closer, the manly scent of his arousal and his spicy cologne surrounding me. I didn't care that he was my therapist. Or that he was my brother's close friend. Right then, *I wanted him in my mouth*. I licked the pre-cum, humming at the taste of him. I flickered my eyes up at him to see if he was watching me as I sucked his bulbous head in my mouth.

"Do it again," he said, his voice low and smoky, that spiraled down from my spine to my core.

He didn't have to tell me twice. With my one hand, I stroked him, feeling his velvety smooth skin bulge and harden underneath my palm as I slowly squeezed his veiny dick. At the same time, I took his tip in my mouth, sucking at it and hollowing my cheeks. He let out a throaty groan and tugged at my hair.

Taking a deep breath and supporting myself by holding onto his thighs, I leaned down and took him inside my mouth inch by inch, kissing and licking every vein and hard ridges. His legs muscles tightened when I flickered my tongue over the underside and felt him bulge inside my mouth.

I let out a loud moan when he spanked my ass, lifting the hem of my dress up. When I was about to pull away, he kept his hand on my hair and said in his husky voice, "No, you filthy little girl. Do what I told you to do. I have been wanting to spank this tight little ass of yours for a long time."

His words made me clench my legs. He gave another sharp spank on my ass as my mouth worked hard and fast on his cock. I closed my eyes, moaning and humming as I took him deeper, relaxing my throat when he took the lead and moved my head over him. My body jumped and shivered when his palm smacked on my burning ass, my underwear dripping wet with my arousal.

"Open your eyes and look at me," he ordered, his voice deep and rough.

I did and groaned with him in my mouth as he gave another thwack on my ass. His lustful, dark eyes were gazing at me. My eyes gleaming with tears as my lips wrapped around him. I hummed and moved my head over him, wanting to please him as my pussy throbbed for him.

Aiden clenched his jaw, one hand tight around my hair and the other massaging the red prints on my scorching ass. I shivered when he lifted my dress, trailing his hand over my spine. I arched my back for his touch. He seemed to like my reaction as a small smile tugged at the corner of his beautiful lips.

My eyes widened, and I moaned when his palm cupped my breast through the thin bra, fondling slowly and his fingers tweaking and pinching my nipple. I squirmed with extreme pleasure, but his hold was firm on my hair, pushing me down on his cock if I tried to pull away from him.

He finally took mercy on me and let go of my breast, trailing his hand over my collar bones, neck, jaw and my cheek. I looked down at his clenching abdomen, the hard muscles of his stomach, the vee of his hip bones when he gently tucked away my hair and brushed his finger over my lips, which were wide open with him inside my mouth, still throbbing painfully.

I watched him with half-lidded eyes and moaned when his finger stayed on my upper lip, feeling my lips sliding over his enormous length. It was so filthy, yet intimate, that I sucked him with more fervor.

"Fuck, Petal, you look so fucking beautiful," he forced my gaze up at him, his eyes on my face. "You don't know how many filthy dreams I've had of you. Bent over my desk, fucking you, spanking you, eating you out. And now that you're here, I am going to take my time fulfilling both of our fantasies."

With that, he slowly guided my head up and down on him, watching him slide in and out of my mouth as I sucked and kissed him in every way I could. I used my hand to fondle his balls, a low grunt eliciting from his throat. The sound of his pleasure was a pleasure to me, and all I wanted right now was to get him off. Again and again, if he would ask me to.

"Oh, fuck, I am going to come in your mouth, Ivy," he gritted his teeth, his hands in my hair as he fucked my mouth; slow, hard, and deep.

Aiden gave out one low moan and jerked when he came inside my mouth. Warm spurts of his seed shooting down my throat as I swallowed greedily. I watched him with tears glistening in my eyes. His hooded eyes watching me and the bob of my throat. He let go of my hair, but I pulled away only to lick him clean from his base to his tip. Humming, I gave slow licks to the flushed head of his cock.

He let out a small grunt of warning and I settled back on my heels, innocently batting my lashes at him, and licked my lips clean.

Aiden's eyes trailed over my face, my tousled hair, my chest and the rumpled state of my dress, my breast almost dropping out of the neckline.

He growled, "Come here."

He held my arm and effortlessly lifted me up on his lap.

8
I DON'T TOLERATE LIES
AIDEN

I caressed the soft skin of her arms, her bare thighs straddling my lap. Mussed waves of her dark hair. I could feel her body trembling over me, the way her hand curled over my shirt, her face hidden in my chest.

If I couldn't believe that Ivy, my little Petal, gave me one of the best blowjobs I have ever had moments ago, then it must be hard for her to believe it too.

Or she didn't expect me to spank her. Or fuck her mouth like that. Or order her to crawl for me...

My large hands glided over her back, under her dress, and squeezed the burning skin of her ass. Ivy whimpered, brushing herself on top of me.

Fuck.

I controlled myself to take it slow, but I didn't expect her to have such dirty and hot fantasies regarding me. I thought I was her silly crush, but not anymore.

I pulled her closer to me, leaving no space between our bodies, and tipped her jaw to look at me. Her soft breasts pressed against my muscular chest. Her blue eyes were shimmering with tears, her lips pink and swollen as she peered at me through her lashes.

"*Ivy*," I whispered her name like a prayer. "Tell me you crawled for me because you wanted to. Tell me you let me fuck your mouth, spank you, because you wanted it too. I need to know."

Her lips parted as she blinked at me, her fingers tightening on my shirt. "Of course, Aiden. I wanted… I wanted all of it." She licked her lips, my eyes lowering to them for a flicker of a moment. "I want *you*."

I shook my head, hearing her confess. *Fuck*. It was a mess, but neither of us could come back from what we had just done. In my own office.

"Did I do something wrong?"

I glared at her and her innocent doe eyes that were tearing up when I was inside her pouty mouth. How could she look like an angel when she had my cock in her mouth moments ago?

"Yes. You made a lot of mistakes, Petal." My husky voice lowered an octave as I continued, "But don't worry, I am here to discipline my filthy girl."

"D-discipline?"

"Of course, I like to discipline—hurt little naughty girls like you." I held her when she squirmed over my lap, trying to find friction. Tsk, poor girl didn't know what she had gotten into. I cupped her jaw, and staring into her eyes, I said, "I'm going to kiss you, Petal."

"I-it's okay," she tried to move her head back. "I-I know guys don't like to kiss after…" she trailed off, looking away.

I frowned. So her asshole ex-boyfriend used her without showing her any affection or after care.

I held her jaw and made her look at me. My voice was soft but firm when I said, "You're right, Petal. Guys don't like to kiss after a blowjob, but men do. Do you want me to kiss you or not? Because I've been dying to taste your pretty lips."

Her cheeks turned bright red as she nodded. "I do."

"Good girl." I pressed my lips on hers.

Ivy melted in my embrace when our lips moved against each other, simply tasting. Her soft breath fanned against my cheek, her hands trailing over the muscles of my arms, bunching the fabric of my shirt before raking through my hair. I licked her bottom lip and deepened the kiss, keeping my hand on the back of her neck, and squeezed her ass with the other.

Ivy moaned, opening her mouth for me as I dived in, tasting her lips, her tongue, her mouth. Even though I had been rough with her, fucking her mouth and commanding her, she touched me tenderly. It was erotic, and hearing the small whimper from her throat, it made me want to do terrible filthy things to her.

My Petal wasn't innocent like I had thought of her. I stayed still, kissing her when she moved her hips over my thigh. Rocking back and forth. The muscles of my thigh tensing when I felt the rough fabric of my pants grow wet with her arousal.

Such a needy little girl.

I tugged at her hair, pulling her back as she gasped. Her lips swollen with the kisses and lust flaming in her sapphire eyes. My dark eyes narrowed at her as she squirmed on my lap. On my thigh.

"Aiden?"

My eyes traveled down to her slender throat. Leaning closer, I licked the soft skin of her neck. Her sweet, musky perfume was intoxicating. She quivered, closing her eyes when I kissed over her beating pulse and moved closer to her ear.

"You are a greedy little Petal, aren't you?" I said throatily, and she stopped squirming. Her hot cunt clenching over my thigh. "Rubbing yourself on my thigh like a naughty fucking girl." I took delight in watching her eyes widen when I held her jaw. "Who told you, you could do that, Petal?"

"I-I am sorry. I just n-needed to—"

My hand lowered to her throat, and lightly wrapped around her pulse, choking her. She bit her lip, wanting to press down on my thigh and relieve the ache in her pussy.

My eyes flickered to her lips, and I asked, "What do you need? Say it."

Ivy turned away, her heartbeat increasing. She must feel embarrassed by everything that has happened. My hand loosened around her throat and I rubbed the pad of my thumb on her bottom lip. She sighed.

I kissed her ear and said softly, "Tell me what you need, Petal."

She shivered, knowing full well I said those same words during our sessions. Every week I would ask her that same question so that she could make goals for the week or the month. I would praise her at the end of the week for completing the said goals or guide her to do better.

Now she would know what I meant by those words.

"I want you…" she whispered and added, "inside me."

Hearing her say it, the words that I wanted to hear for the last few weeks, made my heart feel light. It was her choice, just like it was mine. Having her pressed against me, feel me inside her.

I smiled, kissing her again. I couldn't get enough of her. I hadn't even tasted her, yet I was addicted to Ivy, my little Petal. Her hands clutched the collar of my shirt as if she was afraid that I would move away from her.

Never in a million years, Petal.

"Then you'll get what you need," I murmured against her pink lips, kissing her once more.

Ivy gave me a shy smile that quickly vanished into a small gasp when I turned her over on my lap, her stomach pressing against the semi-hardened bulge with her beautiful ass facing me.

"Aiden?" She looked over her shoulder when I flipped the hem of her dress to her waist.

My palm smoothed over her bare ass, pressing her soft curves closer to my muscled body. Letting her know that there was no escape.

Leaning closer to her ear, I said, "Say the word red if you want me to stop. Nod if you understand, Petal."

She nodded slowly, her eyes wide and cheeks red. That was what my character said in her written sexual fantasies before he hurt her. Hurt her in a way that made her feel alive, cherish her every touch as if he was worshipping her.

I wondered if Ivy felt the same with me. That I was worshipping her tiny trembling body whenever I caressed her soft skin or squeezed her hard enough to leave my hand print.

I wanted to hurt her, cherish her, worship her.

"If you would have told me you want me to fuck you right *here*," I said in my throaty voice, my fingers lightly tapping her sex through the drenched lace, "Then I would have gladly complied with your wishes, Ivy. But you decided to lie. Even after I read your fantasies, you lied to me."

My voice was stern, bordering on angry tone even though I was not angry. I would never touch anyone in anger, especially my Petal. I was disappointed that she never told me how she felt all these years. I forced my attraction and feelings to someone else because I thought she saw me as her elder brother, just like Hayden, and no one else.

She shivered, hearing the tone of my voice, and clenched her thighs. Fucking hell, she was so responsive. If only one sentence could make her wet, I wondered if I could ask her to fuck herself while I told her what to do without touching her.

Ivy squirmed over my lap when my fingers trailed over her, feeling her wetness soaking her underwear. I spanked her lightly.

"I don't tolerate lies. It's rude, and it's unacceptable," I whispered harshly. I spanked her again, a little harder, and cherished the little gasp that came out of her lips. "Especially to your brother's best friend, your therapist, who makes your cunt soaking wet."

"*Oh.*" She made a sound that was a mixture of a moan and a whimper when I spanked her ass again.

Soon, I could feel the coolness of her bare, soft skin, feel her burning sex clench, her legs shivering when I spanked her again and again. My palm scorching with each strike and her ass turning a light shade of pink. Ivy was muffling her moans by biting down on her lip, but I didn't want that. I held her hair and tugged her head back so I could hear the cries of her pleasure and shock more clearly.

I waited for her to say the safe-word, tell me how I got hard on spanking her, scared and disgusted her. But she didn't. She took the spanking like a good girl. I increased the intensity of each slap, hearing her groan loudly when my throbbing bulge poked her in her stomach. She bucked and writhed on my lap, but I was determined until she apologized for lying to me. I heard her cries and her words were nothing but a blubbering mess when she kept apologizing.

"Please, please, please, Doctor Aiden. I am sorry," she whimpered, raising her ass every time I lifted my palm as if she couldn't wait for me to touch her again.

My eyes raked over her beautiful sight, her plush thighs pressed together as if she could hide her arousal from me. Pausing for a moment, I rubbed my hand over her warm ass, slowly massaging the sensitive skin. I would prepare her shower and apply healing lotion as soon as we got back home. If she could bear the thought of touching me again.

Ignoring those thoughts, I loosened my hold on her hair and trailed my hand between her legs. Slowly rubbing my digits over her drenched thong.

"You are soaking wet, Ivy," I said, my voice lowering an octave.

She shivered and pushed her hips back. "Please, Aiden."

I hummed, moving her little underwear to the side and plunged two fingers inside her warm heat, eliciting a loud moan from her. My palm continued massaging her ass gently as my knuckles slid inside her, the pads of my fingers finding the rough sensitive spot and pressing against it. Her body started trembling, and I knew she was close, begging me to make her come.

"Come, Petal. Come on my fingers, you dirty girl," I said, my voice hoarse as she writhed in my lap, my erection throbbing against her stomach while I fucked her cunt. Curling my fingers over her sweet, sensitive spot.

Ivy clenched my fingers, clamping them as I watched her chase down the white-hot lust. A moment later, she orgasmed, coming all over my fingers, moaning my name, squirming on my lap and on the couch.

I was in awe seeing her come apart. So fucking erotic that I knew I would never forget the sight of Ivy, sprawled and limp on my lap from orgasm, her hair mussed, dress tugged over, baring her blooming ass and her juices seeping out of her.

I slowly massaged her sensitive pussy, praising her, and lifted my glistening fingers to my mouth. She looked over her shoulder to see me lick my fingers clean off of her cum, her musky taste burning on my tongue.

This is not enough. I want more.

I pulled her onto my lap, her legs straddling my hips. She

whimpered, feeling my stiffened member rubbing over her sex as I straightened her clothes, caressing her skin, helping bring her back down to earth after the orgasm. Her blue eyes looked hazy as I wiped the tears from her flushed cheeks and ran my hand through her hair.

"You okay?" I asked, raising my brow and utterly pleased myself with the state of her. How wrecked and beautiful she looked. The thought of someone else ever seeing her like that made me want to rage—*no*, she was mine. I'd never let anyone else give her the chance to whisk her away from me. Not when I knew how much she loved being a dirty, filthy girl for me.

She nodded with a dazed look on her face. "Mhmm."

I ignored the fact that she looked away when she replied. I would have to teach her about looking at me while answering me later. Her crush just spanked her, finger fucked her and asked her to swallow his cum. She wasn't okay.

"Are you sore?"

"Sore?"

With my hands on her waist, I pulled her down on my hardened length, rubbing over her slicked pussy. Her eyes widened as she fisted my shirt. "Oh, fuck."

Arching her back, Ivy licked her lips and shook her head. "No, I am not sore. Please fuck me, Aiden."

9
SPREAD YOUR LEGS
IVY

He chuckled, the sound of his low smoky laugh spreading over my body and nestling between my legs. *Fuck, I really want him.* Especially the way his grin lit up his handsome face, the corners of his eyes crinkling, and the way his dark eyes gleamed with pure lust.

Holding my jaw, Aiden brought me close and pressed his lips over mine. He growled, nipping at my bottom lip, "Such a greedy little Petal."

I smiled and pressed myself closer to him, inhaling his spicy male scent and tugging at the curls of his hair. He groaned and pulled me closer, if it was possible, his hands holding my hips and sliding down to cup my ass.

A whimper made its way out of my lips when I felt him grow hard underneath me. I was soaking wet after the spanking, and even after that mind-blowing orgasm, I wanted more.

More of Aiden.

I pulled away when he took us to his table, my legs firmly wrapped around his strong hips. But then I got distracted by his neck and the smooth tan skin. I kissed him below his ear, licking and nibbling my way down his sharp jaw to his collarbone. His hands tightened around my ass, but he didn't stop me.

Aiden put me down on the edge of his desk, pushing everything away. I widened my eyes at him. I couldn't believe he pushed away his notes and diaries for me. He was always organized and kept things in perfect alignment to the point he got annoyed and noticed when someone else touched his stuff. And for him to push off his stationary—

Aiden gazed at me with his gray-black eyes, his lips swollen, his shirt wrinkled and tie undone, with his hard erection poking towards me. I inched backward on the desk, biting my lip when I felt the burn on my ass from his spanking, which amused him.

His fingers grazed my thigh, and I held my breath when he held the hem of my dress and eased it from my arms, throwing it away and leaving me in nothing but my unmatched lace lingerie. His eyes gazed at my body as if he was licking me with his lust-filled eyes, roving over every inch of my skin until I became confident enough to unclasp my bra.

"Let me," Aiden said, stepping closer, spreading my thighs and standing between them to remove my bra with a flick of his wrist and cursing under his breath when his eyes dropped to my heavy breasts.

I busied myself by removing his tie and shirt, trailing my hands over his abs, touching him. He shivered, leaning closer and kissed my neck while he removed his boxers and pants. My back touched the cold wood of his desk as his kisses grew hungrier, flicking his tongue on my nipple and kneading and pinching my other breast.

I gasped when I heard the sound of fabric tearing and widened my eyes when Aiden discarded the two tiny bits of my lace underwear. I watched him bend down, gripping my thighs and pulling me closer so that my bare sex was in front of his face. I bit my lip and reveled in what I was seeing.

Aiden kneeling in front of my spread thighs. It was a dream come true. He licked and kissed my inner thighs, his dark intense eyes flickering up to me and watching me blush.

"Oh—*Aiden!*" I half screamed and half moaned when he licked my pussy to my clit, his tongue flicking and rolling around my sensitive bud as I squeezed my eyes shut and moved my hips.

I had never been touched by a man like this before. No —*not* touched. What Aiden was doing was called devouring and worshipping.

He kissed my slicked lips and licked me, groaning and humming at my taste, which reverberated all over my body, making me cream more. His fingers added to the pleasure as he fucked me while sucking my clitoris.

I let out a small whimper and bucked my hips against his hot mouth, "Please, Aiden, I *need* you."

He pulled away only to lick his lips, lick *my* glistening arousal from his lips. *Holy shit.* "Do you now?" he crooned, teasing me with his fingers and velvety deep voice.

I arched my back, nodding helplessly. "I need you so bad!"

"Then *beg* for it," he whispered, kissing my hip bone. "Beg for my cock, Petal."

I whimpered, hearing his filthy words. When I didn't reply, he went back to teasing me, holding my orgasm on the teetering edge so that I couldn't come. *I knew why he was doing this. I wrote it in my fantasy.* I wanted him to dominate me and make me beg for pleasure.

"I need you, Aiden." I took a deep breath and said, "I need your cock."

He smiled up at me, "You need me where?"

Tease.

"Down there," I whispered.

Aiden raised his brows and tilted his head with a small smirk. "You want me to fuck your ass?"

I gaped and quickly shook my head. *Did he really mean it? My ass—*

"Then where do you need my cock?" He asked, waiting.

Kill me now.

I swallowed the lump in my throat and said, "I need your cock in my pussy. I need you to fuck me, Aiden. *Please.*"

Aiden seemed extremely pleased with my answer as he patted me and said, "That's my good girl."

I flushed and watched him stand up to his full height. All naked in front of me. His broad shoulders, muscled chest, strong thighs and his hardened shaft. I licked my lips, watching him pump himself, wondering how I had managed to deep throat his length inside me.

Aiden pulled me closer, kissing me, urging me to spread my legs for him. I wrapped my legs around his torso, feeling his muscles shift as he moved over me, and then *I felt it*.

The thick head of his dick brushed over my entrance, lubricating both of us as I took a deep breath and held his arms when he pushed inside. I bit my lip at the pinch of pain when he kept pushing until he was fully settled. I felt so full and wet and horny that I never wanted to let go of him, the comfortable weight of his body over me, the way his hot breath fanned over my neck or the way he kissed me. Like the desire of his kiss was more than his desire to breathe.

"Please, move, Aiden," I said, and tried to control my breathing when he looked at me.

"Say my name again," he groaned, retreating and slamming inside me. "*Say. It.*"

"Aiden," I said breathlessly, holding on to his shoulders and scratching his back when he increased his tempo.

His thrusts were powerful and strong every time he went deep inside me, hitting my sensitive spot. I was either moaning his name or telling him to go deeper, harder, or faster. He complied with my wishes and kissed my breasts as I raised my hips to meet his every thrust.

I groaned at his loss when he pulled away. But by the look in his eyes, I knew he had other plans and a second later, I was bent over the desk. *Fuck.*

Gripping the back of my neck, he growled, "Spread your legs."

I did and whimpered when he slammed inside me, spanking my ass. I raised my hands and held onto the edge of the table as Aiden fucked me senseless. His thrusts were either slow and deeper, or hard and fast, alternating in between. All I could do was whimper and moan his name. Take him as he pushed and pulled, spanked and squeezed. I could hear the wet squelches our bodies made when he pushed inside and retreated. Hear the smack when he slapped my ass. Our heavy breathing and how he said my name.

Sex had never felt like *this* before. I didn't know it could be so pleasurable for me and so erotic. I was right in my fantasies—Aiden Stone could *fuck.*

Hell, I was sure he invented the word.

Aiden leaned closer, my back to his chest as he rolled his hips, fucking me and going deeper each time. His hand lowered between us and I moaned, clenching him when his fingers rubbed over my clitoris.

"Yes, sweetheart, that's it, let it go, come for me," he whispered in my ear, his deep hoarse voice edging me as he throbbed inside me, waiting for me so we could come together.

After two powerful thrusts, I was coming with him deep inside me. We both moaned each other's names and stayed still as I felt him inside me. He gently turned me around and kissed me, asking me if I was alright.

I nodded, knowing I needed some time before I could use my voice.

Aiden tucked a strand of my hair behind my ear, his dark eyes marveling over my naked, flushed body. I felt shy of my curves, the urge to hide and cover up increasing with each breath, but it all disappeared when he whispered, "If I could, I would never allow a stitch of clothing on you." His voice was low and smoky. "You're so fucking beautiful, Petal. I want to see you like this, in post-coital bliss, every day."

My half-lidded eyes met his as he brushed his lips against my forehead. *Did he mean it was real for him, as much as it was for me?* I watched him remove the condom, which I hadn't realized he had slipped on without me noticing.

I watched his firm ass when he discarded the condom. I laid back on the desk, wondering if I just got my dreams fulfilled. I ignored the nagging feeling in my stomach, asking me what would happen next. He came back, dressed up in his pants with his shirt unbuttoned, and helped me clean up. I was blushing the whole time, especially when he clasped the hooks of bra for me and winked when he tucked the two pieces of my underwear in his pocket.

"So, I will see you next week?" I asked hopefully after wearing my dress. He was wearing his shirt without the tie, and I could see the hint of tan chest underneath with the small hickey I had given him on his collarbone.

Aiden pulled me closer, kissing me hungrily and leaving me breathless as if to answer me, but the shrill sound of a ringtone made us pull away from the scorching kiss as we blinked at each other, trying to get out of the daze. I swallowed the lump in my throat when he pulled away, frowning at his screen, and told me he had to take it.

I felt bare and cold without the heat of his body and checked the time. Our session had been over for over an hour. Even the sun had set and it was getting dark. His office smelled like sex and musky perfume. His stationery was scattered on the floor and my journal was open on the couch.

"Yes." Aiden's voice was clipped as he answered to someone on his phone, running his hand through his hair. His brows were furrowed, and there was annoyance on his face.

Maybe I should give him space until the call ends.

I patted my hair and stood up on shaky legs, his dark eyes roving over me, making me blush. I shivered, feeling his piercing eyes on me as I packed my bag, flushing more as I picked up the journal and the ruffled pages that started all of it.

"I'll call you later. I have a patient."

I straightened up, feeling his looming frame behind me. Facing him, I braced myself and opened my mouth, but he had to say something too.

"Are you okay, Petal?"

His dark gray eyes were soft, peering at me with a concerned expression on his face. I nodded, clenching my hands in a fist because there was a distance between us. Not just physical but…

Did we make a mistake? Was that all a mistake? Does he regret it?

"Ivy—"

I couldn't bear to hear it. If it was a mistake, I didn't want to hear it when I was feeling so open and vulnerable.

"I should go. I will see you soon." I forced a smile and moved to get my bag and get out of the room, away from him and his intense gaze as far as I could.

Will he regret it and tell me to forget it over the dinner? 'I'm sorry, Ivy. You're not my type. It was a mistake.' Will he be like Jason telling me to lose some weight so I can get tighter, or would he just touch me when he's drunk or high?

A warm hand closed around my wrist, pulling me back.

My lips parted when Aiden cupped my cheek and kissed me softly. The kiss was so gentle that I all but melted into a puddle, warm butterflies flapping around in my stomach as his lips moved against mine.

His hot breath fanned across my cheek when he pulled back and gazed at me with his dark, stormy eyes. "I don't regret anything that we did, Petal. It wasn't a silly, horny mistake. I wanted it. I wanted *you*." His thumb caressed my cheek. "I want you, Ivy. If... if you have any concerns, we will talk about it. We have to talk about it. But not here."

I was blinking at him in shock, surprise and relief when he stepped back, lifted my hand to his face and kissed my knuckles. My heart stuttered at the sight. No one has ever kissed my knuckles and despite whatever we did, that made my cheeks warm.

"We will talk when I get back home, okay?"

I nodded shakily. I wasn't sure that anything was real. He had erased all my confusion and guilt by communicating his wants and needs, assuring me he wanted me. *Holy shit*. Aiden wanted me. My childhood crush wanted me. *Eeeeeppp!*

His gaze turned darker as he said in his velvety voice, "Use your mouth, Ivy, and answer me."

I tipped on my toes and pressed my lips against his cheek. I beamed at him. "I will make your favorite key lime pie and we will talk."

An expression of odd surprise flickered through his face. "Keep doing your daily homework, but write another fantasy with it."

I blinked and nodded as he lightly smacked my ass. "See you at home, Petal."

10
CAN I JOIN YOU?

IVY

I hummed as I finished baking the key lime pie and removed my apron. I checked my phone and saw three missed calls from an unknown number. Jason was using a different phone number to call me while Amanda was a texting me to stay away from her man. I rolled my eyes and blocked her as well.

Zara had sent me a cute picture of Hayden playing with the daughter of Sultan of Azmia. She was only a year old and Zara loved her niece, and so did my brother. I knew they both would make great parents. I still couldn't believe that my best friend was married to my brother and soon I'll be an aunt. I couldn't wait to spoil their baby with delicious sweets and buy them whatever they wanted.

I hummed and kept my phone aside as it was time for Aiden to come home. My grin was wide when the bell rang and I eagerly opened it without checking who was on the other side.

A beautiful woman stood on the porch wearing a silk dress and high heels. Her golden hair was glowing as she stared at me from head to toe and I was aware of the stark difference between us. I was wearing a frilly summer dress and my hair was mussed since the afternoon I spent with Aiden. My mascara must have clumped and started smudging while her makeup was flawless.

"Is this Hayden Knight's residence?" She asked, her voice soft and feminine.

I had the sudden urge to clear my throat before I reply. "Yes, he's my brother. Who are—"

"You must be Ivy!" She smiled, holding her hand in front of her. "I'm Addison. You've grown up since I last saw you."

My heart dropped to my stomach hearing her name and slowly shook her cold hand. She invited herself in, walking past me and looking around. She smelled like a lobby of a luxurious hotel, and I was sure the handbag she had was more expensive than my tuition.

I gingerly closed the door behind me and followed her to the living room..

"Is there a reason you are here?" I asked, trying to be polite. But I knew deep down I disliked her. I have always disliked her, and I knew she knew that, too.

Addison was Aiden's fiancee—ex fiancee. They both were high school sweethearts and I remember how she always clung to Aiden's arm whenever I saw them together. I had seen her flirt shamelessly with my brother whenever Aiden wasn't around. They broke up a few times but somehow always ended up together.

When Hayden told me Aiden was proposing to Addison, I was sad, but relieved. I was dating Jason at the time and I thought my silly childhood crush was going away and Jason might propose to me soon. How foolish I was.

Addison tilted her head at me and pulled out a small mirror and gloss from her handbag. "I came here to talk to Aiden," she said, moving her hair over her shoulder and applying a lip gloss. "I have something important to tell him."

Her eyes flickered to me as she shut the compact and I had to suppress a shiver at how cold they were.

"Don't worry, Ivy. I won't take too much time." All her movements were graceful and elegant, making me very aware of how I was fidgeting with my fingers in my lap. "So, how's your college? I heard you're majoring in business."

She was trying to make small-talk, so I indulged in it.

Thankfully, I heard Aiden's car and knew he was home.

Aiden

"Guess what I found on my way back here, Petal." I had a small smile on my lips as I closed the main door behind me and looked at the box of macaroons that were Ivy's favorite.

After my call, I knew she was uneasy. I had to make sure she knew we were on the same page about what we had done. I still smelled like sex and her and fuck, it was the best feeling ever.

I wanted to fuck her again.

"Aiden."

My smile slipped off at hearing that voice. I stayed frozen in the hallway as I looked at her golden hair in perfectly coiled waves, her face sharp and eyes cold as she titled her head at me and the box in my hands.

"What the fuck are you doing here?" My voice was harsh enough to make anyone flinch, but it didn't work on Addison. It never did. She would need a heart and emotions to know that I left her because I was angry at her, disappointed and miserable in our so-called relationship.

"Addison said she wanted to talk to you." My eyes flickered to Ivy. Her wide blue eyes seemed concerned as she stood up from the couch. "I'll be in my room."

"It won't take long for her to leave." I glared at my ex when Ivy left us alone. I ignored her gaze on me as I kept the box of macaroons on the kitchen island. I stared at the key lime pie and crossed my arms, facing her. "What do you want?"

"I'm pregnant."

My brows furrowed as I stared at her face and her stomach. I clenched my jaw and wondered if she... *no*. Not with her, but what if she was?

"Whose is it? Because last time I checked, you were having sex with more than one person in our relationship."

"We were engaged, Aiden."

I chuckled and slid my hands in my pockets. "We *were*, Addison. I want you to take the paternal test. I always used protection."

Her gaze narrowed as she walked around the house and I hated that Ivy let her enter—*wait*. "How did you know I was here?" I had packed my bags after finding her with her boss in our penthouse, and left, leaving my ring on the coffee table. I had blocked her number and made sure she could never contact me again.

She hesitated, looking at me from the photo frames that lined on the wall.

"I had Hayden's address saved on my phone."

Of course she did. Hayden had warned me two years ago on that ship that she was hitting on him, but I had ignored it, thinking alcohol had something to do with it, but I was so fucking stupid and naïve. Hayden had warned me that she was with me because of my money, but I was too much in love with her to ever believe that.

"His sister is still cute," she commented and pointed to a picture that had all three of us, me, Ivy and Hayden when we were kids.

"Addison." I didn't want her under my best-friend's roof. Didn't want her anywhere near my sweet Ivy. "Do you know who the father is?"

She straightened up and looked at me with her unflinching stare. "I wanted to let you know before—"

"Before taking a paternal test? That was your stupid fucking plan? You think I'd come back to you just because you're pregnant?" I took a deep breath and calmed down. "I want you to take the paternal test tomorrow in the morning. If you don't, I'll have my lawyers call you."

Her eyes widened and cheeks flushed as she walked towards me in her high heels. Her dark dress was silk and looked expensive. She didn't look like Ivy. She didn't smell like vanilla or dress in oversized clothes and fidget with her fingers when she was nervous.

Fuck.

What the hell was I thinking?

Of course, Addison is not Ivy. Then why the hell was I comparing them?

I must have hit my head somewhere.

"You can't call lawyers on me. I am here for you, Aiden." Her cheeks were flushed and her voice was turning high pitched. "Please, just hear me out. What you saw that day w-with Jeremy…"

I took another deep breath and answered, "Did he coerce you into sleeping with you?"

She remained silent.

"Did he hold your hand, force you to enter the entrance code of our penthouse and have sex in our bedroom that we were sharing for two years?" I asked, despite knowing I had seen the surveillance footage of them making out in the elevator, then in the hallway, before she smiled at him and pulled her own boss with his tie in our penthouse. "Oh, I'm sorry. I saw you riding him and moaning his name on the couch we bought together while my ring was on your finger."

She shook her head, tears gleaming in her eyes.

When she remained silent, my gaze fell on the floor. "I

was willing to go to relationship counseling with you." A laugh made its way out of my throat before I looked at her shocked face. "I know. I was stupid enough to consider counseling for both of us... trying to save the engagement, but then I realized I never loved you, Addison."

"But I loved you, Aiden!"

"We were foolish kids in lust. Nothing more. I don't remember how you look without makeup, when we had our yearly anniversary, or what you even like to do for fun. We never went out for dates and dinners, and when we did, it was for the show. Either for your parents or for some fashion gala."

Addison blinked at me, shaking her head. "N-no, no, I remember we went on dates, Aiden. We... we loved each other in our own way."

"Then why did I feel so miserable in our relationship? Why did you cheat on me?" I shook my head, a headache forming in my head. "I've had enough of you, Addison. Please leave and never see me again."

I let her wipe her tears as I stared at the television, remembering the movie night with Petal. I wanted to hold her. Caress her soft skin and ask her to talk to me about silly things so I could hear her sweet voice for hours.

"Do you love her?"

I looked at Addison, her pursed lips as she stared at the frame and gave me a sad smile. "I meant Hayden's sister. Ivy. You always called her by a special nickname when we were in high school. Petal, right?"

My jaw clenched as she continued, her voice low, "I was always jealous of her. I knew she was just a kid, but the way she looked at you as if you were her entire world, as if you could never do anything wrong, keep her safe. A Prince Charming—she still looks at you the same way, you know." *I know.* "She was so sweet, always baking extra cookies for me, even when I was so jealous of a kid just because you loved her so much."

I froze hearing her confession.

"And I thought I could never compete with that." A small sob tore out of her lips as she wiped her tears. Her nose and cheeks were flushed. "I could never compete with what you and Ivy had—*have*. So I tried to love you, show you all my perfections and hiding all my flaws because I didn't want to lose you too, Aiden. When taking you to Denver wasn't enough, I hinted at our future and you proposed to me the next day. You are a foolishly loyal man, Doctor Aiden Stone." She chuckled weakly, and taking a deep breath, she faced me. "But now you need to be that loyal to her because she deserves it."

Addison took out a paper from her purse and handed it to me. "I'm sorry, I lied to you."

"What?" I unfolded it to see the test included her name as mother and her boss's name as father.

"I know who the father is, I just wanted to… I don't know, see your reaction and I was right. Sorry for that." She caressed her stomach, ignoring my glare. "It is Jeremy's, but I'm not sure if I'll keep the baby. I came here to say goodbye and… you don't have to worry about ever seeing me again."

My eyes widened, "Addison, are you—"

She smiled and shook her head. "No, you need to learn to leave your therapist's brain in the office. I am moving to London. Better job opportunity."

I nodded, processing everything she had said. She was moving on and leaving the country. Even though we had used each other for money, status, and sex, I felt relieved to know she would be okay on her own. *Maybe I can email her a list of therapists when she gets settled in London.*

She kept the familiar ring box on the kitchen island. The one I had opened in front of her on my knees.

"You better treat her right, Aiden." Her voice was broken. "Or I will tell her brother. I've heard he's a Prince now, so you have to watch out."

"I will treat her right." My voice felt heavy and I couldn't help it. I pulled her closer and hugged her one last time. "Take care of yourself, Addison."

She sniffled and stepped back, smiling at me. "I will. Goodbye."

I watched her walk out of the house with her chin high, and I knew she would be alright. Leaning back on the counter, I sighed.

That was a long ass day.

I should talk to Ivy. I have to talk to her.

Knocking on her door, I opened it and found her room empty. The shower was running, and the door was ajar. My cock pressed against the confines of my pants as I thought of her naked body showering in the warm water.

Being a gentleman, I knocked on her bathroom door and heard her squeak, which made me smile. "It's Aiden, Petal. Can I join you?"

She didn't reply for a few seconds and I frowned, wondering if she heard me.

"But I am naked."

"And your point?"

"You want to shower with me?"

"Yes. Preferably without clothes."

"C… come in."

Ivy didn't need to tell me twice.

11
GOOD GIRL

IVY

"I prefer the lilac color."

"Of course, you do."

I pouted and batted my lashes at him, but he booped my nose and said, "Be good." Aiden walked over to see another curtain.

We were in IKEA, shopping for furniture and the necessary stuff for Aiden's new home. After joining me in the shower, completely naked, he had conditioned my hair when I told him I already shampooed it and asked—no, ordered me, to stay steady and keep my back arched when he kneeled on the bathroom floor to eat me out. I would have slipped and gotten a concussion when I climaxed in a couple of minutes if his arm hadn't held me.

When we had finally walked out of the shower and got dressed, he told me he wanted to celebrate with me for getting a new home.

"You bought a house?" I was excited. Very excited. So much. But it meant not having him at Hayden's house more often. It meant no sharing breakfasts or dinners or showering together or sleeping with him on the bed after watching a scary movie together.

"Yes, Petal," he squeezed my hand on the dining table. "I…" Heat crept up his neck, and I was shocked to see Aiden Stone look nervous for the first time in my entire life. "If you're free, you can come over tomorrow and… stay? If you'd like."

I didn't know what to understand after hearing him.

"You want me to come over tomorrow to your empty new house and stay with you?"

"Yes. No." He raked his hand through his hair and looked at me, really looked at me. "Yes, I want you to stay with me. In my house. Together. In different rooms if you prefer, but yes. And you don't have to answer me right now because we need to tell your brother about our relationship, and it can seem—"

I waved at him, scrambling out of my chair, "Wait. Wait. What? Tell my brother? Relationship?"

He leveled my stare. "Ivy, we didn't have a one-night stand—"

"Technically, it was afternoon."

"Do you want to get spanked again?"

Yes, please.

He held my hand and pulled me between his thighs. It was cute yet hot how we both smelled like my body wash, but he had his own male scent clinging to him that I wanted to wrap around him like a leech.

Aiden continued, "I am serious about this, Petal. I want to bend you over this table and fuck you deep and whisper all the degrading things in your ear that make your pretty face flush. But I also want to wake up with you tomorrow in the same bed and make you breakfast, then go to buy groceries together because we really need to—there's no salt in this house."

I chuckled and stepped closer to him. His large hand pressed against my back as he pulled me over his lap, his fingers tucking my hair behind my ears as if he wanted me to see him. My cheeks flushed under his sweet, gentle gaze. I couldn't even look him in the eye. So I focused on his collarbone and said, "I am serious about this too, Aiden. I mean… you read all my embarrassing fantasies."

"Mhm, I did. It was very hard not to resist you after reading how my thick, girthy cock stretched your sopping wet pussy."

"Stop teasing me."

"Never, Petal."

He was grinning.

Groaning, I hid my face in his chest as he pulled me closer, kissing my hair. "If we are both serious, we need to tell your brother."

"He will be mad."

"At me. But you matter more than his silly protectiveness."

I kept my focus on my thumb that was caressing the stubble on his sharp jaw. I shivered, thinking about that same stubble brushing against my inner thigh moments ago.

"What if we hide it from him?" I asked, "I don't want you two to get into stupid fights and I know you both will."

"Sweetheart, let me take care of him. If he finds out about us from someone else, it will hurt him more."

Aiden was right. "Fine, we can tell him tomorrow. After you show me your house."

"Hm, I'd need your help with some things."

I frowned. "What things—*oh!*" I half-gasped and half-moaned when he pulled me over his bulge, holding my hips.

"We can talk about it later, Petal. Help me with this thick, gritty problem that was caused because of you."

"Shuddap." I kissed him, feathering my fingers through his hair as he moved me over his hips.

That night, we slept together naked in his bed.

Huffing, I followed him, stomping my feet as much as an adult can get away with, "Excuse you, I am good."

"*Hm.*" His brows were furrowed in a cute way as he checked the curtain, reading all the descriptions printed on the label.

Who checks the label of everything? Apparently, the tall therapist I'm infatuated with.

"Don't *hm* me, I am," I raised my chin and pointed to the lilac curtains. "You should get these. Or something pastel like—"

"Like the pink underwear you're wearing?"

A shiver of pleasure rolled through my spine at hearing his dirty words. He always had a way to make me blush just by a look or a few words. It made me embarrassed and flushed.

"I-it's not pink." I looked away from him, and remembered we needed to get book shelves, bed and—

His hand wrapped around my wrist and dragged me with him. I frowned at his back, which was clad in a white shirt with sleeves rolled over his forearms. What the hell happened?

"Are we not getting the curtains? Or the book shelves? Bed?"

Aiden shot me a dark look and pulled me closer to him. "I don't care about the curtains, Petal. What I care about is punishing a dirty girl who keeps lying to her therapist, *hm?*"

My face flamed as we walked to the parking lot, the sun looming on top of our heads. My feet were already wobbling, wondering what he was going to do. Aiden opened the passenger door for me and I sat down on the warm leather. I felt the dampness of my thong.

"What do you mean by punishing?" I asked, my voice breathy when the car started with a purr.

"Remove your underwear," he commanded, his gray eyes daring me to disobey him, and one small part of me wanted to disobey, see what he'd do if I didn't move.

"You do it." I didn't know where the confidence to look him in the eye and answer him came from, but I was loving the way he looked amused with a small smirk on his lips.

"Say please. Haven't I taught you any manners?"

"N-no. I..." My legs clenched when his fingers brushed over my bare thigh, tickling the sensitive skin of my inner thigh. I watched his hand hovering over my thigh, and I had to suppress the urge to hold it and press it down on my skin that was burning for his touch.

"Stop whimpering and say please, Petal. I'll touch you and remove your soaked underwear." His tone was playful, and I knew he was teasing me, delighted by how easily my cheeks turned red at his playful words.

Scrunching my hands on the seat, I whispered, *"Please."*

Pleasure coiled tightly in my belly when he touched me. Seeing his hot, large hand on my left thigh made me cream even more. I bit my bottom lip when he squeezed my skin, trailing his hand over my thigh.

"Hold your skirt and lift it for me." He ordered, his voice rough and velvety that made me want to squirm.

"W-what if someone sees?" I stuttered, my pulse hammering loudly in my ears as I held the hem of my skirt in my fists. We were still on the road and I trusted Aiden, but I'd never done anything like that before.

"Then let them see." He looked at me, his eyes hooded with lust. "I want everyone to know my dirty little girl was lying and is getting punished for it."

I squeezed my eyes shut and lifted my skirt to my waist.

"Hold it up and open your eyes."

I shook my head, scrunching the material of the skirt.

"Quit being a brat and open your eyes. Now." There was an edge to his voice, and I knew not to test him.

Taking a deep breath, I opened my eyes and held the hem of the dress to my chest, shivering at the coolness of the air conditioner on my bare skin. I pressed my legs together.

"Good girl," he praised me, squeezing my thigh softly, and it made my clit throb. I wanted him to praise me more.

"Now tell me which color are your panties, Petal." His tone was serious, but it seemed like he was talking to a child.

"It's pink."

"Show it to me."

"What?"

My eyes drifted to his sharp jaw, to his eyes as he maneuvered the car smoothly on the road while I was still holding the hem of the skirt. Exposing myself.

Aiden flickered his eyes on me, on my thighs and looked at me. "Remove your underwear and hand them to me."

I looked out of the window at the road and asked in a small voice, "R-right now?"

"Do you want more punishment, Petal?"

Yes, Doctor Aiden. Ignoring that filthy thought, I lifted my hips and wiggled them to slide down my thong. My hands were shaking when the fabric lowered to my sandal heels and I handed it to him in his palm.

I felt lighter, on the edge, and he hadn't even touched me.

My lips parted when he felt the wetness with his fingers and pocketed the thong in his pants. "You are such a wet, needy girl," he said and pressed his fingers on my bottom lip. I greedily sucked on his fingers, licking my cum from them and humming at the taste. He rasped, "Good fucking girl."

I whimpered when he pulled away his hand, but that whimper turned into a soft moan when the same fingers pressed over my clit, slowly rolling the sensitive bud and toying with it.

"Shh, stay still. I don't want you to come so soon." He whispered as I rocked my hips over his hand, rubbing myself over the pads of his fingers, getting them slicked, but he never slid them inside me like I wanted him to or got me to the edge.

"Please, Aiden," I was whining and begging, humping his hand when he kept the slow pace of rolling my throbbing clit with his fingers.

He groaned, looking between my legs. "Fuck, Ivy, you are so fucking wet, I can hear you. Smell how wet your cunt is." He lowered his fingers, and I moaned when he slid one digit inside me. I clenched him tightly. "Don't you fucking cum, Petal."

"Please..."

My voice trailed off when he fucked me with his fingers, his thumb on my clit. Lewd sounds of my wetness surrounded us with my soft moans. The scent of my musky feminine arousal hovered in the air and seeing his forearm flex with veins as he moved his finger inside me made me want to—

"Don't cum. If you do, I'll make you lick your own mess." His voice was angry and hot and I would have orgasmed if he hadn't withdrawn his fingers from me to make me lick them clean.

I was so distracted that I didn't even notice when we had reached his house.

Aiden tucked my skirt down as he parked the car in the garage and removed my seatbelt. "You okay?"

I shook my head, angry at him. "I was so close."

"That's your punishment, Petal." He kissed my forehead, tucking a lock of hair behind my ear. "You don't always get what you want. Especially when you lie."

"That was just—"

I groaned when he got out of the car and followed him.

"I'll keep your panties for today, and keep your pussy bare for me, will you? I want to keep you on edge until I get to fuck you." He smiled at me as if he hadn't just said those filthy words, kissing me and showing me his empty new house.

* * *

AIDEN HAD SHOWN me the pool in his backyard and looked into his fridge to see if we could cook something for dinner. Despite being slightly mad at him for not making me cum and teasing me during the entire tour by giving me vivid explicit details on exactly how he was thinking of christening his house with me, I wanted to talk about him the day before.

"Aiden."

I was seated on one of the stools of the marble kitchen island, as the house didn't have any furniture except the kitchen stools. He had mentioned that he would get an interior designer to get his place furnished unless I wanted to help him without any distractions. I agreed. We were not a couple who could buy cutesy bedsheets together without thinking about stripping and having sex.

When he looked at me, he closed the fridge. He must have known I was serious just by seeing my expression. He walked towards me and asked, "What happened?"

I looked at my hands and took a deep breath. "I wanted to ask about Addison. Is everything okay?"

I had known from my brother, Hayden, that Aiden had broken up with his fiancée a month ago. They had been together since they were in high-school although they had broken up and got together several times.

Aiden sat beside me on the stool and his face was soft

when he said, "Yes, everything's okay. She's pregnant, and she came to tell me goodbye."

"Oh."

There was a moment of awkward silence between us.

"I found her with her boss in our bed. I... I left and didn't see her again until that day."

"Aiden." I held his hand and peered at his face. "I didn't know she cheated on you. Were you angry at her? When you saw her yesterday?"

His thumb rubbed over the back of my hand, making soothing patterns on my skin. "I was angry at first, but then we talked. I got my closure, and I think she got hers. I think that's really the only reason she came to see me."

I smiled at him and kissed his knuckle. I frowned when his eyes turned cold as he said, "But if I see your ex-boyfriend, I will punch him. He's a dickhead for sleeping with your friend who's your roommate, no less. Your brother wanted to call his old friends and have the poor kid abducted and threaten him, but I vouched for a punch."

I let out a soft chuckle, shaking my head. "I'm glad you vouched for a punch, but you don't have to do anything. It hurt a lot seeing him with Amanda, but in a way, I was relieved." I continued when he tilted his head to hear more. "We started dating because he sat beside me during Business Accounting and talked to me, wanting to know if I would be at his birthday party. Next thing I know, we are hooking up and he wanted to be together. But he never truly cared or showed any interests in my hobbies or... *me*. I don't think boyfriends tell their girlfriends to lose weight after se—"

"He did what?" Aiden's eyes had gone dark, his jaw clenched.

I swallowed and shook my head, "I-It's nothing, he just..."

"It's not nothing, Petal," his voice was firm. "He told you to lose weight after you slept together?"

I couldn't meet his eyes and nodded. Feeling ashamed and embarrassed all at once.

His warm hand closed around my hand and his voice was much softer when he said, "I'm sorry. I don't want to push you to tell me about him when you're not ready."

I looked at him, at his furrowed brows and the small frown on his lips. That was his concerned but angry face. Aiden was angry... yet gentle with me. I had told him about my childhood in his clinic and he never once got angry, just took some notes and talked me though it.

But now... he seemed furious. He wasn't being a therapist right now.

"I-I'm ready. I talked about it with Zara... I can talk." He gave me a small nod, so I took a deep breath and continued staring at his large hand that covered mine. "He'd often do that when he couldn't, you know, come from sex. He was usually drunk when we got intimate and told me that l-losing weight would make m-me tight."

Aiden's hand squeezed mine as my voice wavered and broke. My vision was blurry, but I was not sad. I was angry that I let a guy like him treat me that way.

"He never took me out on dates or showed any love. He wasn't a good boyfriend and I'm sad and angry that I stayed with him." I sighed and squeezed Aiden's hand. I had said everything without sobbing like I did with Zara on call. It was easier to talk about difficult things with Aiden. "I am glad it's over and I'm glad I came back to San Diego, and you opened the door."

"Me too, Petal." His face was unreadable, but he pulled me closer, cupping my cheek and leaning in for the kiss.

But his doorbell rang, making both of us jump. I looked at him in confusion and followed him to the hallway when he opened the main door.

12
WHAT IF
IVY

"Hi!"

"Uh, hello."

I stood beside Aiden and waved at the girl who was holding a box of—

"These are cupcakes." She shoved them in Aiden's hands and smiled at both of us. "I'm your neighbor, Mia Miller. Nice to meet you."

"Aiden Stone," he said firmly. "This is Ivy and—" His phone rang in the kitchen and he offered an apology to both of us, "Sorry, I've got to take that."

As soon as he was out of the earshot, Mia looked at me and said, "Your husband is so hot!"

I shook my head, heat creeping up my neck. "Aiden is not my husband."

She raised her brow and looked at the man on the phone in the hallway and back at me. "He wants to be, by the way he was looking at you."

I turned redder. She looked a few years younger than me, with shoulder length dark hair and bright green eyes that twinkled with mischief.

"Mia!" someone yelled her name, and it was amusing to see Mia turn red when she turned around to see a handsome man near an expensive, sleek car. "I brought your favorite pudding."

"No need to yell, James. I'll be right there."

James was dressed in a suit, even in the heat, and walked inside the house next door. He seemed good-looking enough, but by the way Mia was gawking at him and rubbing her goosebumps, it seemed that he was special to her.

"And that was James. As you saw." She chuckled nervously.

"You like him."

"*Wha*—I don't even…" When she saw my straight face, she sighed. "It's a silly crush. It'll go away when I get older."

Ha, that's what I thought too, but look at me!

"How old are you?"

"I'm seventeen, which my father likes to remind me every time when my friends sneak in some beer cans during sleepover." Her phone started ringing, and she pulled it out from her pocket to see the collar ID and rolled her eyes. "Speaking of, my father invited you two for a dinner on the weekend. A warm welcome dinner for being our neighbors, he said, but I'm sure it's his plan to be geek about his antique collection. Feel free to bring your earplugs!"

I chuckled and noted the dinner date as she sprinted to her house, patting her hair down before entering her house. I was glad that the neighbors were friendly and Aiden would fit right in. So would I, when I move in.

"Who was on the phone?" I asked, walking into the living room and finding Aiden pacing with a frown on his face as he typed on his phone. "Did something happen?"

He shook his head. "It was from the hospital. I was checking up on a patient who was sexually harassed. Make sure he is okay during the investigation, but it was pushed for later."

I knew Aiden was listed as a clinical therapist in a hospital, but I never understood the true grounds of it until hearing those words. Listening to patient's trauma, their sadness, grief, anger and guiding them to their better mental health must have been hard. Especially when he had to leave for work on his off day.

"Will you be okay?" I asked him.

Aiden gazed at me and smiled. "Don't worry about me, Petal, I'll be okay."

I trusted Aiden and knew he could take care of himself. If he was not okay, he would have told me. So I nodded, squashing down my anxiety.

"Who was that girl earlier?" He asked, pocketing his phone.

"That was Mia. She's your neighbor's daughter. Very bubbly!"

He tugged me towards him, surprising me. Aiden was a very touchy and clingy person and I loved every moment of it. "You mean our neighbor's daughter, hm?"

I swallowed, gazing at his obsidian eyes, and nodded. "Yeah."

His hands lowered from my waist to the skirt underneath it and squeezing my ass, making me gasp and arch against him. "I have been thinking..." he started, leaning closer and pressing a wet kiss on my neck, his hands groping me everywhere. "I want to fuck you in every corner of this house."

My hands scrunched over his shirt as he pushed my back against the island, his expert fingers getting rid of my clothes.

"That's a lot of sex," I said, breathing heavily when I was in nothing but a bra and a skirt. He still had my pink thong and thinking back to his hot demeanor made me rub my thighs together. Aiden noticed it and bent down to scoop me over his shoulder, making me yelp as my world turned over.

"Aiden! What are you doing?" I cried out, holding on to his back for dear life. My hair swayed as he took me upstairs.

He spanked my ass and said, "Fulfilling my promise, Petal."

I gasped when he threw me over the bed and before I could take a breather, he was on me. The new mattress dipped with his weight as he crawled over my body, claiming my lips in a starving kiss. I moaned into his mouth and removed his shirt, undressing him as he made a quick work of removing my skirt and bra, leaving me naked.

My shyness crept over when his dark eyes roved over every inch of my bare skin. My first instinct was to hide, but I suppressed it and tried to keep my chin high and show him I wasn't insecure anymore. His gaze softened when he cupped my cheeks and kissed me. I melted into the sweet kiss and fluttered my lashes at him when he pulled back.

He moved my hair over my shoulder, caressing my neck and jaw and said, "I want to play a game, Petal."

"Game?"

"Mhmm," he hummed, lowering his hand to my left breast and rolled his finger around my nipple, making me shiver. "I get to please you. Make your pretty pussy flutter and cum every time you say something nice about yourself."

My eyes widened, surprised and confused. I felt embarrassed that—

"Shh," he tugged lightly at a lock of my hair. "Stop overthinking, Petal. You're a good girl and I want to hear you say it."

"I'm a good girl?" I said, my cheeks turning red, and I had the sudden urge to hide.

"That's right. You are." Aiden was smiling and seeing that smile, I'd have done anything he asked but... "Keep going."

I frowned when he pushed me on my back, settling himself between my legs and squeezing my breasts. I whimpered when his hot mouth wrapped around my nipple, licking and biting it.

"I...I like my baking," I blurted out, and Aiden rewarded me with hickeys on my breasts. I was flustered, but I said, "I-I like how my breasts look."

He groaned and pulled away to weigh them in his hands and said, "I fucking love your tits, Ivy." His eyes darkened when he looked at me, "I'd be lying if I didn't confess how I dream about fucking them, painting them with my cum and keep you marked with my scent like an animal."

My lips parted at the intensity of heat swirling in his eyes, how he kept planting more kisses and hickeys all over my stomach, holding and caressing my curves. I was turned on and a bit embarrassed when he made me say more nice things about me. If I didn't say anything, he'd stop touching me. Aiden was a tease through and through.

"I like my hair," I whined when the tip of his cock brushed over my wet slit, his eyes pinned on me. "Please, Aiden! I can't think anymore. Fuck me."

He chuckled, the sound erotic and deep. "I haven't even fucked you yet and you're already fucked out of your mind, Petal?"

I scowled at him. "You have been teasing me for hours and if you don't want to, then I will use my hands—"

"Like hell you will," Aiden growled, grabbing my wrists before I could lower them between my legs and pinned them over my head with one hand.

I bit my bottom lip when he teased me again, hovering above me, and said, "I didn't tell you to stop, Petal. I can do this all day."

"I like my eye," I said harshly when he finally plunged inside me, making me gasp and moan. "Oh, fuck."

His pace was steady, making me say more things and keeping me on edge until he was satisfied and letting me cum when I said 'I like how soft my thighs are.'

"You're being such a good girl," he whispered in my ear, tugging at my hair. He had turned me on my stomach, facing the mirror on the side of a bed. It was so hot to see Aiden looming behind me, fucking me slowly and watching his abs and body tense and move in such detail. My skin was flushed, eyes glowing and lips swollen with kisses.

"Now look in the mirror and tell me something you like, Petal," he said, keeping his pace and caressing my back.

"You," I said, meeting his eyes in the mirror's reflection. "I like you, Aiden."

He stopped, heat creeping up his neck as he grabbed my jaw and kissed me, slamming inside me. "I like you too, Ivy. So fucking much," he said, increasing the base and pulled back as I whimpered, grabbing the mattress when he fucked me into the bed.

"Tsk, look at yourself," he grabbed my hair, tugging at it until I was looking at our reflection again. "Look how sexy you are."

"I-I am sexy," I stuttered, my eyes glistening speaking those words. His thrusts turned deeper and harder. "I am beautiful."

"Yes, my sweet girl. You are sexy and beautiful, Ivy," he whispered, rubbing his fingers over my sensitive clit.

I exploded with pleasure and so much love for the man who whispered more sweet and filthy things in my ears. White hot lust blinded me as I kept coming and crying out his name again and again.

When I came back to Earth, Aiden was tugging me towards him. "You did so well, Petal," he whispered, kissing my forehead and moving hair out of my face. "I'm so proud of you."

My eyes were still teary as he wiped them away, kissing my cheeks. "I've never felt that way before," I confessed and wondered why there was a sticky—"Oh."

There was cum on my breasts.

Aiden's cheeks were red. "I'm sorry, I couldn't control it seeing how pretty you looked when you orgasm."

"Oh." I said and touched it, rolling around my breast. "Okay."

I heard a growl and looked at Aiden, who was sporting a semi. "S-stop doing that, Ivy."

I smiled, enjoying the way I could tease him so easily. "Why not, Doctor Aiden?"

He narrowed his eyes, and he was about to retort when his cell phone started ringing. He excused himself with a swift kiss on my lips, making me smile. I was still in bed, catching up on my breath and staring at the ceiling, when he came back with a small frown.

"I'm so sorry, Petal. I've to go stay with the patient for the investigation—"

I sat up and grabbed his hand, kissing his knuckle. "You don't have to apologize, Aiden."

He looked conflicted, and I knew he wanted to stay with me, cuddle and take a shower, but his job came first. I liked how passionate he was about his work.

"I can drop you off at Hayden's—"

"I'll take a cab." I kissed his lips and fixed the collar of his shirt, stepping back. I didn't want him to take a detour. "Now go do what you do best."

He smiled down at me and my heart stopped and started with a pounding beat when he wrapped his arms around my waist and kissed me again. "I won't be late," he promised, pulling away, leaving me breathless and cold without him.

What if Mia was right? What if... I wanted him more than just... No.

I needed to slow down.

13

CAN I JOIN IN THE HUG?

AIDEN

"Why are you so late—*oh*."

I watched Ivy's blue eyes widen when she glanced beside me.

"Hey, Bug," Hayden grinned, looking at his little sister who stood at the doorway. Zara, the Princess of Azmia and fiancée of my best-friend waved at Ivy.

Ivy didn't miss a beat and lunged in her arms and hugged her as much as she could with a huge bump between them. I had asked Hayden in the car if they were having twins, and by the look of horror between the couple, I knew my answer.

Hayden had called me when I had left the hospital. I had to suppress the guilt that surged when I saw his name and his annoying selfie on my phone. He and Zara were arriving early and wanted me to pick them up from the airport.

I wondered how he would react if I told him that I like Ivy. More than like her. He would be stupid not to notice my attraction towards her for all these years. He had warned me and his friend groups that she was off-limits to us, always glaring at any male acquaintance she had. He was protective of her, and I could understand his reasoning. Their father didn't care what happened to them as long as they were alive. Hayden could live without their love, but not my sweet Petal. Hayden had been the only one to offer her any sort of sibling love.

"I missed you so much," Ivy mumbled, hugging her brother. I smiled at them, Hayden's light brown hair falling on his forehead as he kissed his sister's hair. I gave them some space and walked inside the house as the royal guards followed me in their dark suits with the bags of the royal couple.

After the recent events in Azmia, Hayden and Zara were forced to have two guards around them all the time, but since they were living in Hayden's house, they were allowed some freedom from the guards.

"Aiden," I turned around and slid my hands in my pockets when Hayden stepped inside his old room that he would share with Zara. "Did something happen between you and Ivy?"

I didn't reply, knowing I couldn't lie to him.

"Did you find any name for the baby?" I asked.

He narrowed his blue-gray eyes at me. "Don't change the subject." But it worked. "No, we haven't decided yet. Zayed, the Sheikh of Azmia, and the biggest pain in the ass, made an entire presentation why we should name our child after him."

"Huh, that seems eventful." He seemed happy, despite the mild annoyance. Every time he glanced at Zara, he had an odd, vulnerable look on his face, as if he couldn't believe she was with him. "You look happy. You should've got together sooner with her."

Hayden scoffed, "You are the one to say that after dropping my phone in the Indian Ocean."

I remembered that. Two years ago, after he had been whipped by some beautiful lady in Azmia for the night, he had been checking his phone constantly. Even after boarding the ship, as we left the country together. We had a small fight, and we both watched in pure amusement and horror when his phone fell in the Indian Ocean. He had been so frantic that he was ready to jump into the ocean to grab his phone or even command the captain to stop the ship until he could get the phone back.

Just for the hope that she, aka Princess Zara, would call back.

"Well, it worked out way better, don't you think?" I teased as Zara waddled in. She was slim and tall, but with the huge bump, she looked like a little penguin.

"I hope I'm not disturbing any precious bromance."

"No, your highness," I said, bowing my head because she hated being addressed as that. "I already have someone that I prefer."

"Do I want to know who it is?" Hayden asked, raising his brow as he held Zara's hand when she sat down and started putting a pregnancy pillow on the bed, books, water, and a dagger on the nightstand.

Before I could open my mouth and tell him the truth, Ivy called us down for the dinner.

I left them to freshen up and decided that it would be best to be honest about my intentions with Ivy and Hayden. I didn't want to sneak behind my friend, my only friend, to kiss her. I wanted him to know I was serious about her.

"What are you thinking about?" Ivy whispered, watching her serve delicious lasagna on four plates. The royal guards had checked the house and, after confirming it was safe, they were staying in the house across the road. Ivy had cooked extra and gave them the food as well. She was too sweet.

I lightly held her arm, her eyes peering at me. "We should tell Hayden."

She faced me, shock and surprise flickering on her face.

"What would we tell him, Aiden? That we had sex in your office."

If I still had arms after talking to her brother, I would use them to give her a lesson for speaking like that. As if it was just sex for her.

"Yes, that and how serious I am about *this*," I said. "I don't want to hide it from him."

Ivy bit her bottom lip. "I don't want you to regret it."

I wanted to embrace her and assure her that I meant what I said, but we both heard footsteps coming downstairs. I kept the plates of our dinner on the dining table as Hayden ruffled her hair, asking her about her studies. Zara wanted to know more about Ivy's ex so she could give him a lesson, but Hayden calmed her down. It was strange yet nice to see the Princess of Azmia threaten Ivy's ex with the most vulgar threats while being graceful.

During the dinner, when Hayden asked about the therapy sessions, Ivy seemed more than happy to talk about it. How it helped her and how she was getting praised for fulfilling her assignments.

I cleared my throat. "Because of some reason, my friend will take over her therapy sessions from now on."

"What?" Ivy asked, "Why? You are… you are perfect. I feel more comfortable with you."

Zara looked between us, and judging by the twinkle in her eyes, she knew.

"My friend is more than capable of helping you, Petal." I kept my fork down. "I cannot be your therapist anymore."

"Why?" Hayden asked.

"Personal reason."

"What personal reason?" Ivy said, pouting.

Fuck, I want to kiss that pout.

I raised my eyebrow at her. I couldn't be her therapist anymore because we, or at least I, had feelings for her. Not to mention we engaged in a sexual relationship in my office. I couldn't be her therapist anymore, even if I wanted to. It would be wrong.

"Do you really want me to say it out loud, Petal?" I asked with a small smirk.

"What is it?" her brother bit out.

"Your little sister and I—"

Ivy blurted out, "I had sex with Aiden."

"I knew it!" Zara beamed, clapping her hands, unaware of the tension hovering in the air.

Hayden and I looked at Ivy, her hands covering her mouth as she muttered a little *oopsie*. I moved in time to avoid getting stabbed in the eye when Hayden threw a fork at my face.

"Are you trying to blind me, you dick!"

"You touched my little sister!" Hayden stood up and so did I, but I wasn't fast enough to avoid his punch. He was one of the best Navy Seal for a reason.

I staggered back, feeling the throbbing pain in my left cheek and jaw. I could hear Ivy yelling at him to stop, scolding him for punching me.

I swear I heard Zara say, 'Hayden looks hot' as she scooped some more lasagna on her plate.

"But you are my little sister!"

"That doesn't mean you can order me with whom I decide to have sex with or not!"

"B-but... Aiden? Out of everyone you could have... *Aiden!*"

"This is for throwing a fucking fork at me," I said and breathed out. He faced me, his face burning with anger. I didn't give him time to use his block before punching him.

"Can you guys please stop fighting?" Ivy asked, glancing between her brother on the floor and me.

"He stared it," I said, pointing at him, who was trying to choke me.

"Because he had sex—"

"Oh, for fuck's sake, grow up!" Ivy yelled at both of us, silence falling around us. I watched her breathing heavily, her eyes watering as she looked between us. Even Zara stopped eating and looked at all of us with her doe eyes.

"This is the reason I never confessed my feelings for Aiden. Because you always warned off every guy around me, especially *him*," she said to Hayden, her voice cracking.

Oh, God, no. I didn't want to make her cry.

"Now look at you two, bruised and fighting over me. I like Aiden, and having sex with him was my choice. If either of you don't like the sound of it, I will leave for university tomorrow and stay in the dorms."

Hayden clenched his hands, his anger reeling off of him. I could see the conflicting emotions in his eyes, the tick of his jaw.

"I like her, Hayden," I said, knowing that I might lose my close friend. "It matters to me that you believe me because you know I can never lie to you."

Zara stood up and gently held his fist, entwining his hand with hers. He wiped the little blood from his split lip. "Is that why you had sex with her?"

"It was a mutual decision."

Glaring at me, he glanced at his sister, who was silent. "Do you like him, Ivy? The way you will reply to my question will affect my friendship with him."

"Hayden, it doesn't have to—" she protested.

"No. If you give him the power to break your heart, I will end things with him."

"Quit being dramatic," I sighed, "Answer him, Petal. You know the answer since we met."

Hayden's eyes widened, looking between the two of us, his face scrunching. "I might barf."

"There, there," Zara muttered, rubbing his back.

Ivy's face flamed. "Nothing happened between us like that until that day in the office."

"I don't want to know!" Her brother complained, covering his ears.

Ivy peered at me, her blue eyes soft. "Yes, I like Aiden."

I smiled at her, controlling the urge to kiss her, praise her for accepting the truth in front of me and her brother.

"Gross," I faced Hayden, shaking his head at us in disgust. "You both are gross. Already doing all those weird eyes."

Crossing my arms, I said, "Should I tell her what gross stuff I have witnessed being your friend?"

Zara raised her hand. "I want to know."

Hayden shot her a glare and looked at me accusingly, "You mean the stuff which you later joined in and lick—"

"Okay," Ivy piqued. "I am going to bed. Nice talk. Come on, Zara."

"Ivy," Hayden called out and hugged her. "I know you like him and he is my friend, but I am here whenever you need to talk. About anything."

"I am here for you too, Hayden," she replied, hugging him back. Zara joined in to the hug and it looked so sweet, I got FOMO.

"Can I join in the hug?" I asked.

"Yes!"

"Absolutely not."

Hayden glared at me when I joined in the hug.

14. SWEET

AIDEN

"Is that him?" Hayden nodded at the lanky guy with mussed blond hair, laughing with a group of girls before walking away.

"Yes," I said, crossing my arms as we watched Jason walk away from the library. "She deserved so much better."

Hayden glared at me. "She still does."

"Hayden, shut the fuck up and help me up." We both turned towards the Princess of Azmia, who had threatened us to let her tag along with us. She was sitting comfortably in my car's back seat, but it was not much use since her guards had followed her to Ivy's university in a sleek black car which was gaining a lot of attention from the students.

"I don't know why you had to come with us, Princess." Even though he wanted his fiancee to stay with Ivy and have a girl's day, his tone was soft and I knew secretly he was glad that he could keep an eye on her. He was not only protective of his sister but also his soon-to-be-wife.

"I wanted to kick him in his balls, but a good threat will do," she huffed out, supporting her back as I nodded at Hayden.

All three of us followed Jason as four guards followed us from a distant. I sneaked ahead to corner the asshole and seeing the confusion on his face made me want to do terrible things to him.

"Who are you?" He asked, sizing me up and trying to stand taller when I was a head taller than him.

"I'm Ivy's boyfriend," I said, hearing Hayden pretend to barf in the background. "I promised her I'd punch the shit-head who—"

Jason chuckled. "Nice lie, she's too… you know. I bet she paid you to do this. You're not her type, anyway. She likes guys like me who treat her like a bi—"

I punched him before he could finish and shut his mouth before he could scream. I yanked at his collar, ready to break his nose, but Hayden held me back. "If you call her, message her, or even dare to think about her again, I'll make sure that you can't use that garbage mouth for more than just a week."

"Aiden."

I glared at Jason as I pushed him away. His small cry was disgusting as he covered his mouth. "What the fuck?" He said to himself, while he should be thanking me for not breaking any bones.

"You should've provoked him instead," Hayden said, pulling me to the side. "That way you can—"

"Where's Zara?" I said, and we both turned around to see Zara glaring at Jason and saying something to him. I was in awe when she unsheathed the small dagger in front of his face and Jason fell on his knees, begging for his life.

Satisfied, Zara sheathed the dagger and started waddling to us with a wide grin, a dimple on her cheek.

"I can see why you fell for her," I said to Hayden, who was gawking at his fiancée before rushing to her side and asking her if she was okay while the kid she threatened was shivering on his knees.

Maybe I should have let Zara handle everything from the beginning.

Ivy

"That was not nice, Petal." Aiden's deep voice brushed through my ear, his body pressing against my back. I whimpered, his sharp face staring at me through the reflection in the mirror. "Teasing me like that. Wearing this skimpy dress."

I nodded, too embarrassed and flustered to say anything. *How could I?* He had lunged at me when I had tried on the dress, wrapping his hand around my throat and shutting us both in the cramped place of the dressing room.

"Aiden," I breathed. "What if someone finds us?"

When I had told him about going to buy a dress for Zara and Hayden's wedding, I didn't think he would want to come with me shopping for a dress. He must have important work to do, but he offered to come along, telling me it was another reason to see me all dressed up in different clothes and then unwrapping me from them as if I was his personal present.

Aiden pulled back, turning me around. He wasn't letting me go. No, he was removing the dark blue tie he was wearing. My legs clenched, arousal seeping out of me. Anticipation coursed through me because I knew what was coming next. After dating for more than a month (despite my brother's whining, who thought we wouldn't date for more than a week), I knew what Aiden enjoyed when it came to physical activities.

"Hands, Petal," he said, his voice firm and his dark eyes gleaming like a predator who had trapped his prey.

Swallowing the lump in my throat, I extended my wrists towards him. Leaning down, he kissed the soft inner part before wrapping his tie around them, binding them together in a knot. I squirmed, extremely turned on, knowing he would tease me and reward me soon.

His large hand cupped my cheek. "If you don't want to be caught, then you have to be quiet, Petal. You will be quiet, won't you?" He purred in my ear, my toes curling.

I nodded, peering up at him. Gasping, I held my breath when he wrapped his hand around my throat, raising his brow at me. The light of the dressing room cast a shadow on his face, making him look stern.

"Y-yes, Aiden. I will be quiet," I voiced it out, knowing he wanted me to say it. Consent to it.

"Good girl. Now turn around."

I followed his command, holding my breath when he kept his hand on the back of my neck. My eyes were on his reflection in the mirror, watching him tug at the short dress which barely covered my ass. I flushed red, looking away when he lifted it up to my waist, baring my nakedness to him.

Jumping, I tried to muffle my yelp when he spanked me. "I can see your soaking cunt when you bend over, Petal. Is this what you wanted to wear to your brother's wedding, hm?"

There was something definitely wrong with me for getting turned on by his harsh words, his anger.

"No," I said. "I just wanted to tease you. See you... angry."

Aiden met my eyes through the mirror and gave me a small smile, his hand rubbing the burn on my ass. "I know, Petal. You are a little brat that I love to tame," he said, his hand lowered to my dripping sex and patted it lightly, making me gasp.

"Spread your legs."

I did, trying to support myself on the mirror with bound hands. But he held me, his firm hand on my neck and other holding my hip. He would never let me fall. I trusted him.

I wasn't prepared when Aiden lowered his zipper and slid

himself inside me in one powerful thrust. I groaned, his hand clamping on my mouth when he sighed on my neck, the front of his shirt pressing against my back.

"Stay quiet, you naughty girl," he whispered. "Don't want to get caught, do you?"

I shook my head, his hand on my mouth lowering to wrap around my throat, making me look in the mirror as he reared back and slammed inside me. I bit my lip to muffle my moans, but it was too much. I had to bite down on the fist of my bound hand to try to hold my groans and whimpers when Aiden fucked me senseless.

The wet slaps of our bodies echoed around the cramped dressing room, the mirror rattling with us. Aiden clenched his jaw, forcing my cheek on the mirror and using his hands to hold my hips and going faster. I shivered, my legs trembling at the pressure of release.

"Not yet," he hissed, spanking my ass and reminding me who was responsible for my orgasm. "I swear to God, Ivy, if you come right now, I will cum inside you and walk you to the parking lot like this. Without any underwear."

"No," I whimpered, clenching around him at his filthy words.

He tsked, slowing his rhythm when his hand lowered to my clit, rubbing me as I squirmed and whined. "Such a dirty girl to get turned on by that. Do you want to walk out like this, Petal? With my cum dripping down your thigh, hm?"

I couldn't answer. Blood had rushed to my cheeks, my breasts aching and pleasure bubbling inside me when Aiden kept teasing me. Kept me on the edge. Toying with me with his words.

"Don't be mean," I said, my eyes teary. "Let me cum, Aiden."

He fucked me, spanking me again as he whispered, "But you like me mean, Petal."

I nodded. *I did.*

"Be a good girl and beg me to make you cum," he said, not moving inside me. Stretching me and watching me squirm around his girthy length.

"Please make me come, Aiden. Please, I... I need to cum badly," I blurted out. "I will do anything, please, please, please."

"Anything, hm?"

I nodded, not caring about my words.

"You and I are going to have a lot of fun at your brother's wedding, Petal," he said, devilish smile curling at the edge of his lips when he started moving inside me.

For a moment, I wondered if I had made a deal with the devil, but then I was falling, climaxing with him deep inside me as I squeezed my eyes shut. I felt him release inside me, the hot spurt curling my toes, his body going lax behind me while he touched me tenderly.

"Are you okay?" He asked, his voice soft as he ran his hand through my hair.

I managed a nod, biting my lip when he pulled out. I shivered, noticing the way his dark eyes watched the cum leak out to my inner thigh. "Aiden," I whispered.

He flickered his eyes to me and smiled, "Sorry, it's a turn on to see you like this. Thoroughly fucked and sated. If I could, I would always keep you like this."

This man is not human.

"Let me clean you up," Aiden offered, removing the tie binding my wrists and the skimpy little dress that I had picked up on a whim to tease him with.

After arguing with him for buying all the dresses that I had worn (even the one he fucked me in), I was pouting on the way back home. I could buy my own clothes, but he would never listen to me.

"Stop pouting, Ivy," he said, changing the gears. "I wanted to buy you the dresses, so I did."

"I didn't want you to pay for them."

"I wanted to. And if I want to splurge on you, I will," he said, his voice firm as we reached Hayden's house. "You said you would do anything if I made you cum, so I will pick out what you wear on the day of the wedding, understood?"

I huffed, crossing my arms and looking away from him. "So fucking bossy."

"I heard that." Grabbing my jaw, he made me look at him. His pupils dilated as he said, "Don't be a brat and wear all of it."

"And if I don't?"

"Then I will discipline you."

"Stop smooching in front of my house and get in here!" We both jumped away hearing my brother's loud voice, shouting from the front door. Aiden winced when he hit his head on the roof of the car and rubbed it.

"I hate your brother," he said, glaring at his figure.

"The dinner's getting cold, kids," Hayden replied as if he knew what Aiden had said.

I picked up a bag of the dress while Aiden picked the other two as we made our way towards the front door. "Just a few more days. We are going to Azmia together, so you have to hold out for a few days," I smiled and continued, "I know you secretly love him."

"Whatever." Aiden scoffed, opening the door for me. "You know I love you more."

My heart stumbled hearing him say it so casually, he was so unfazed by it. Then it made sense. We had known each other for almost half of our lives and shared vulnerable fears, secrets and even flaws. He had counseled me as my therapist and listened to me as my boyfriend when I wanted to vent. We knew each other, understood each other.

"Yeah," I smiled as I held his hand. "I love you too."

Aiden's eyes widened for a moment before he pressed his lips against mine. The kiss was gentle, soft and easy. Just how love should be. It was perfect.

We all had dinner together and talked to Zara's family through a video call. We would be leaving with the royal couple in their private jet soon and stay in the Golden Palace until the wedding. Zara had made a special desert for all of us called *kunafah* and it was delicious, melting on my tongue with each bite.

"It's so sweet!"

My eyes widened when Aiden kissed the corner of my lips and winked at me. "Not as sweet as you are, Petal."

THE END

READ EXPLICIT BONUS SCENE HERE
Or type this link into your browser:
https://BookHip.com/ZKDJJWX

Thank you so much for reading Twisted Therapist! If you enjoyed reading this book, I would be grateful if you could leave a review on the platform(s) of your choice.

Reviews help other readers like you find this book and are hugely appreciated by authors!

Love always,
Mahi

EPILOGUE

IVY

"Believe it or not, she can now boil the water without turning on the fire alarm system," Mia's father, Clyde Miller, said proudly while Mia pretended to shoot an imaginary bullet through her finger guns into her head.

I chuckled at her and warmed up to the family of two... including James, who was busy in a telepathic conversation with my boyfriend. They looked awkward with squinted eyes and one-worded answers. I wanted to ask what was wrong with Aiden, but he was seated across me.

"Sooo..." Mia started, noticing the stare-off between the two men. "Tell me how you bagged Mister Aiden over here."

That got Aiden and James' attention as both men looked at her questioningly.

"Bagged?" Aiden asked, frowning at me.

"She's asking how we got into a relationship," I explained the term in his language.

"No." Mia shook her head, her eyes sparkling with mischief, "It means where she found you and which cheat codes she used to—"

"Mia," James warned, his voice deep as he gave her a stern look.

Her cheeks flushed as she took another slice of pizza. I still couldn't figure out the relationship between the two. James and her father were good friends, and he often visited them because James was the CEO of an architectural firm where Mia's father worked. Mia's mother had passed away and her father was her only family, but he had done a brilliant job at parenting because she was funny and sweet.

"Ivy is my best-friend's sister," Aiden answered Mia's previous question, shooting a small smile in my direction. "We met after a few years and it worked out for us."

"Holy shit!"

Both Clyde Miller and James said in unison, *"Language."*

Which she ignored—*attagirl*—and continued, "So you are living the dream of a brother's best-friend trope. That's so cool! I can't wait to tell Summer about this."

I hid my blush and stuffed my mouth with more pizza. Apparently, her father was going to cook a big meal for all of us, but he had forgotten to go to the grocery store and we ended up ordering pizza. I had baked cookies and Aiden had brought an expensive white wine, which we all enjoyed except Mia, who had sulked in her chair. But I had seen James pass her a few sips and shook his head when she wanted more, keeping the wine glass away from her reach. It was cute.

When the conversation turned from our relationship to our works, the men started talking about working in hospital to private firm and to James' company, Fox Constructs. I'd heard the name before. It was one of the first companies in the States to use green engineering.

Mia's head snapped up from her cell phone when James announced his resignation.

"Wait, what do you mean by leaving Fox Constructs?"

He looked at her and said, "I'll be teaching a course in design in Saint Helena."

Her eyes went wide, and I was so intrigued by their conversation, I gulped down another glass of white wine.

"Since when?" She asked, her voice high pitched. "Why Saint Helena out of all the schools?"

From what I remembered, she went to the same private school. Although calling it a school would be a shame because it was built like a five star resort that included school and a university with three buildings on a huge plot.

James shrugged, "I always wanted to try teaching and what better way to start from basics of designing to young minds."

"No," she said, standing up from the table.

I was about to pour another glass of white wine when Aiden held my hand and gave me a stern look. I poked my tongue at him but stayed put because I knew he didn't want me drunk for our... nightly physical activities.

"Mia," her father frowned at her. "Sit down. It's not a big deal."

"You knew about this and didn't tell me?" She accused her dad and seemed hurt. Crossing her arms, she glared at both the men. "I need some time to process this. It was nice meeting you, Ivy and Aiden."

She left the dinner hall, and we all heard her soft footsteps walking away. Her father sighed, and I almost jumped in my seat when Mia came rushing back, taking James' glass of white wine with her and running away, yelling about how she deserved it. I pursed my lips to stop the bubble of laughter and faked a cough.

"She is a nuisance," James muttered under his breath, but I knew he was hiding an amused smile.

"My nuisance," her father said lovingly. "She's just like her mother. Please excuse her behaviour. She's not like this on most days."

"It's okay, Clyde. She's a sweetheart. We are happy to have you as our neighbors."

* * *

"I want your P-E-N-I-S inside me," I slurred and smiled at Aiden when he cradled me against him. Like a baby. His baby. "Am I your baby?" I poked his cheek, giggling when he glared at me. We were moving up and down and my stomach was acting funny. "I want to suck your boo-boo."

"For the love of God, Petal, please shut up." Aiden laid me down on a cloud of comfort and I squirmed, making a snowman on the cloud. "This is why I told you not to drink white wine. You have such low intolerance."

"Meanie," I pouted at him when he knelt on the floor and removed my sandals, softly holding my feet. I was ticklish and almost kicked him in his face when he removed another sandal.

"Too bad you love this meanie," he whispered and settled my head on the pillow.

I shook my head, "No."

"No?"

"No. I only love Aiden... he's—he's really cool. Handsome and grumpy but—" *hiccup*, "—he sex me so good. *Dabs.*"

"Dabs?"

I took a deep breath and glared at the man, who looked so much like Aiden, and nodded. "The best. Bestest. I want to marry him."

I heard him take a sharp intake of breath and before I floated into the dreamland, I heard Aiden's voice whisper in my ear, "Marry me, Petal."

By the time I fell asleep, I had a huge derpy smile on my face.

Continue Reading the first 5 chapters of Tempting Teacher

MY BUTT IS CUTE

MIA

My best friends were liars. There's nothing fun about being in a cramped, sweaty house bursting full of teenage hormones, loud music, sweat, alcohol, and the burning sharp smell of weed that hangs in the air.

I elbowed my way through the sweaty mob of drunk people and looked for my friends who were eager to try Aaron Matthews' 'new stuff' in his room. It was his house and being the rich kid of the governors of our state meant he could do whatever he wanted when his parents were out of town.

As our school was starting tomorrow, everyone from our year, including the seniors, received a video invitation—yes, a video—to come to his party and get 'smashed.'

I know, kids these days.

"Hey Mia!" I turned around and came face to face with Aaron, the host. His pupils were wide and the whites of his eyes were red.

"Where's Emma and Summer?" I yelled at him because the music was too loud.

"What? Who?"

"Emma and Summer? One of them is dressed as Sailor Moon because she thought this was a costume party." Summer was the only person who would come to a party dressed in a blue skirt and white top with red thigh-highs. Emma had sighed and muttered she doesn't know her when she came to pick us up with her driver. "Are they upstairs?"

Recognition lit his eyes as he nodded. "That blue miniskirt chick? Yeah, she bought a lot of candies. But I don't know where they are." He leaned closer. The smell of weed wafted in my nose as he said in my ear, "My room is empty. Do you want to come over?"

I shook my head. "No, thanks. I don't do drugs."

Turning around, I walked away from him before he could finish his next sentence. I froze in my track when I saw a girl, probably a senior, squealing and running from the kitchen hallway towards the backyard in nothing but denim shorts with her hands covering her... girlie bits.

"I think I've seen enough for a day," I muttered to myself and called Emma for the tenth time in an hour. I shouldn't have agreed to Summer's idea of going to this party, but her puppy eyes were enough to convince me.

The shrill sound of sirens rang through my ears, and my eyes widened. The DJ stopped the music and everyone started scrambling.

"What's happening?" I asked the tipsy girl beside me and helped her up when she tripped.

"Cops are here," she grinned dizzily at me. "The party is moving to Caleb's house, you should come with us!" Cheers went off as the crowd rushed towards the backdoor.

A neighbour must have filed a noise complaint, but if the cops saw us all with drugs and candies—as Aaron liked to call it—we would all be in big trouble. And it was not in my bucket list to get arrested by cops and see the disappointed look on my father's face when he bails me out and then disowns me.

I dialed Summer's number.

"Hello?" Her honeyed voice spoke through the phone.

"Summer! Where are you guys? The cops are here—"

"Ha!" she snickered. "You fell for it, dummy. Send me a voicemail after the *beeeeep*."

I sighed, listening to her mimic a robotic beep and mentally noted to scold her for changing her voicemail. Again. "Call me when you get this. I hope you and Em are safe with Caleb."

Caleb was Emma's boyfriend, and I hadn't seen him run through the panicked and excited crowd of drunk teenagers from the backyard. I was too short and petite to push through the incoming teens and go upstairs. My body was already being pushed through the throngs of people as they all laughed and shrieked in drunken glory. Panic seized me when I heard the cops barging into the house from the front doors, and adrenaline coursed through me with the fear of being disowned by my father.

I stomped and elbowed out of the crowd, running in the opposite direction of the people, sprinting down the other street and thanking past me for wearing run-down Vans and not heels. My heart burned as I took a few deep breaths, trying to calm myself down. I was alone on the empty street.

Then I remembered that my friends could have gone to Caleb's house for the afterparty.

Stupid, stupid Mia.

To make matters worse, rain started pouring, instantly soaking me and my clothes. I cursed, trying to pull the thin blouse from my skin, but it was stuck to me like a glue. I almost called Dad and remembered that he was going to watch a hockey game with his friends and how much he was looking forward to it. I didn't want to disturb him.

That left only one other option. But it's a weekend and he could be on a date, and what if I'm disturbing him, too? Shaking my head, I stood under the shade of a tree. Cold water sluiced down my hair, falling on my crossed arms and making me shiver. I averted my eyes when a pair of two men walked past the other street, eyeing me.

I remembered his words from before. When I had walked downstairs after getting ready for the party. He had looked at me with a frown and said, "Call me if anything happens."

Anything includes getting stranded in the rain, right?

I dialed his number, rubbing my arm to stop the goosebumps. My fancy blouse and shorts were drenched. I didn't want to imagine how my face looked with mascara running down my cheeks.

He picked up on the third ring. His rich, velvety voice purred through my ear, "Where are you?"

Biting my lip from smiling, I rocked on the soles of my shoes and asked, "How did you know I'm in trouble?"

"Are you in trouble?"

"No."

"Then should I go back to my date with Julia, who's waiting for a very special dessert?"

Irritation pricked through my skull, and I regretted calling him. I should've gone to Caleb's house like everyone else. "Oh, shoot. I'm sorry for disturbing your date."

"I'm kidding." Relief poured through me, and I hated that it relieved me when it shouldn't. He was my father's bestfriend. It *wasn't* right. "Tell me where you are."

I told him the street name and heard the keys jingling and the door slamming shut through the phone.

"Stay there, princess. I'll be there in ten."

The sound of his smooth voice soothed the panic, and I stayed still even when the rain got harsher. Tiny prickles of shiver climbed up my spine as the rain dribbled faster. I jumped when thunder struck the dark sky, goosebumps skittering all over my body.

I rocked back and forth on my shoes, my heart beating faster as I waited for his car to show up. It was way past my curfew, and just before I could call him again, my phone died.

"This is great," I muttered underneath my breath and bumped into something. My head shot up, and I blinked at the guy standing in front of me. "Sorry."

"Who are you?" I tried to walk beside him, but he held my elbow. His voice was slurred, and he seemed drunk. "What are you doing out here at this hour… wearing *that?*"

"*Excuse me?*" Frowning, I struggled with his hold on my arm, but his fingers tightened on my skin to the point of hurting. "Who the hell are you, trying to hit on an underage girl at this hour?" I clenched my jaw and pulled away, but he didn't budge. "Let me go or I'll scream and kick you in your family jewels so hard that you'll never be able to procreate."

"So you're underage, drunk, and all alone in this rain, drenched in your skimpy top?"

"Thanks, Mister Obvious, but I'm not drunk."

"You're coming with me." The leering smile on his face made me want to puke.

"No, I'm not." I knew kicking him in his balls wouldn't work as he was already dragging me away from the street where I told James I'd be waiting, but I could stomp on his feet as hard as I could.

"Let her go."

I sighed in relief at seeing him standing in front of me. Rain had stopped pouring for a while and the only sound I could hear was the loud hammering of my heart against my ears and my breathing.

"I found her first," the stranger said with a disgusting smirk on his face. "You can get in line."

My jaw dropped hearing his crude words as heat creeped up my neck. I did the only thing I could do. I pinched him. *Hard*. The guy squealed in a high-pitched voice and let go off my arm.

"Disgusting prick." I rubbed the red marks of his fingers on my skin.

A warm coat hugged my shoulders, and I glanced at his sharp face leaning close. "Are you okay, Mia?" His deep blue eyes were concerned and a little angry.

I nodded, too afraid to speak anything at such proximity to his face. His fingers brushed over the red hue on my arm and glared at the guy who was too busy to notice James' sharp look.

I stifled my gasp when he prowled towards him and punched him so hard that he fell down. James held the guy by the collar of his neck and there was blood on the corner of his lips. He said something to him. The stranger's eyes flickered to me in fear as he nodded and James let him go. He scampered away without looking back at us.

"What did you do?" I asked when he grabbed my wrist and took me to his car. I knew he was rich, but I didn't know he was I-can-buy-as-many-electric-and-sports-cars-as-I-want rich. So count me mystified when I saw him unlocking the car door with a card. "What did you tell him?"

His eyes narrowed at me, and I felt the nerves tighten in my belly. He hadn't shaved for a day and the scruff on his jaw looked, dare I say, delicious under the lamplight of the street.

"You have five seconds to sit in the car."

I'll sit wherever you want me to sit, James.

Ignoring the rubbish in my head, I said, "And if I don't?"

"You can walk home, can't you?" He cocked his head to the side.

He wouldn't, would he? I didn't want to bump into another pervert when I walk back home. But he came to my rescue the second I called him and it's a weekend. He could've just called an Uber for me, but he didn't.

Calling his bluff, I scowled at him and raised my chin. "You'd never let me walk home alone at night."

"You're right," he growled, stepping closer and crowding me against the back of his car. He seemed angry before, but now, he looked furious. So furious that he could eat me. "I'd never let you walk home alone, Mia, but I *can* and I *will* let you walk home trailing with my car if you don't put your cute little butt in the car right fucking now."

I don't know why, but I found that extremely hot.

Once again, I was ignoring the rubbish my brain was sprouting out.

He said my butt is cute.

Yep, there was definitely something mixed in my drink.

"I-I want to know what you told that guy."

"Five."

My eyes widened and I pulled his coat closer, getting distracted by his smoky cologne. "You can't do that."

"Four."

"I'm not a kid!"

"Three."

"Are you even listening to me?" I asked, glaring at him.

"Two."

"You know what?" I leaned closer and licked my lips, giving him his coat and thrusting it in his hands. "You can keep this if you want to keep treating me like a child. I'll walk back home on my own."

I turned away from him, walking away.

"*One*." His smooth voice sent a chill down my spine, "And wrong answer, Princess."

YOU'RE HOT

MIA

"And wrong answer, princess."

I swallowed the lump in my throat when he neared me, his tall height looming over me. He seemed so put together, I hated it. Absolutely *loathed* it. I was soaked from my head to toe and my shoes squelched when I moved while he looked untouched from the rain. There I was looking like a wet sock while wearing wet socks, and he looked like he just walked out of an Abercrombie cover shoot.

"W-what are you going to do?" I did not mean to stutter. Stuttering was for the weak, but I'd be lying if I said his closeness didn't affect me. And he smelt so, *so* good. I wanted to bury my nose in his neck and sniff. Even ask about the cologne he used so I could buy it like a little creep and spray it all over my bed and roll around in it.

Yep. There was definitely something in my drinks.

"I'm going to fuck you."

"What?" My lips parted as a car zoomed by and wetness seeped out of me, making my already wet underwear *wetter*. "You sure… you want to do that?" I looked around the empty walkway, my cheeks feeling warm.

"Of course I'm sure, Mia." He sounded so assertive and stern that it scared and excited me.

It was no surprise that I had the biggest, fastest, and juiciest crush on him since my father introduced him to me a year ago. I was too busy stuffing my food with the wedding cake when he had showed me the fine specimen that was James Fox in a fitted tailored suit. With an awkward, braces-covered, toothy smile and insecure body, I had shyly shaken his hand while he ruffled my hair. *Ruffled.* Like I was a kid to him. Probably was, considering he was eighteen years older than me.

At sixteen, I had filed my attraction towards him in the celebrity crush folder of my brain along with Cillian Murphy, Michael Fassbender, Andrew Garfield, and Tom Hiddleston. I realized that I had a thing for hot older men with British accents, who possibly looked British, too. No biggie, lots of people have crushes on older celebrities, and it took me one look at Tumblr's homepage to notice that.

But my crush on James was anything but simple.

James held my elbow, his grip firm and my skin singed where he touched me, and pointed to the passenger car seat. "*Sit.*"

I craned my neck to look at him and licked my lips when his eyes met mine. "W-what would my father say?"

I almost cringed mentioning him in all of this. I did not want to think about my dad when I was with James, which was very little, but I had to be sure.

If my dad found out his bestfriend slept with his only daughter... *yeah, no, it won't look good.*

He raised a brow, making me scuffle in my shoes. "Your dad doesn't need to know about this." His fingers tightened on my skin as he moved closer, our clothes almost touching. "Now sit in the damn car before I drag you in there."

My dad doesn't need to know?

He *wanted* me to be his dirty little secret.

My tongue felt like lead. I scrambled to the car seat and sat down, trying to calm my heavy breathing, but it wasn't working. All I could think about was his large, veiny hands touching me everywhere, bringing me on the verge of orgasms again and again while he fucked me like he said he would.

"Why are your cheeks red?"

Because I'm having very R-rated thoughts about your hands, tongue, and cock inside me.

"Because I'm cold?" I hid my face behind my hair, hoping he wouldn't notice I now resembled a tomato.

I held my breath when his fingers touched my jaw, making me look at him. His brows were furrowed as his eyes danced over my face, and then he touched my forehead with the back of his palm.

"You're hot."

"Well, I hope so," I replied with an awkward chuckle.

"What did you drink at the party?" he asked, surprising me by leaning closer. I parted my lips to answer, but I got lost in his dreamy eyes. I couldn't muster any thoughts when he was near. *How was I going to be intimate with him when my brain had turned into puddle? Was I even ready for that? With him?* I was pulled back to earth when he pulled the seat belt over me and strapped me in.

Oh. He wasn't going in for a kiss.

Yet.

"I don't remember," I answered, looking down at my lap and cringing at the thought of my wet clothes soaking his expensive leather seat. "I'm sorry for ruining your car seat."

The car started with a smooth purr just by a press of a button. He flickered his eyes at me and replied, "Don't worry, I get the covers changed every week."

How rich was this guy?

"Why every week?"

His lips curled at the corner. "Because they get stained —*ah*, ruined every week."

I frowned at him. *Ruined by what?*

Shrugging, I leaned back on the comfortable seat and looked out the window, my heart rate increasing with each mile. By the time I noticed the familiar road, I was shivering.

I had to make sure if he really planned to fuck me. Maybe he thought he would give me a start-of-the-high-school-as-a-junior gift by taking my virginity and showing me all the ways of pleasure and desire. He sure looked like sin and I was willing to be his sinner, even on my knees if he asked me to.

But there was one other thing...

"James," I started when he parked the car in my driveway. "I'm seventeen."

He slowly blinked at me. "I know."

Oh, wow, talk about determination.

"I am really seventeen, James," I emphasized. "Like not adult but kind of adult*ish*. I mean, I will be eighteen soon, *haha*, not that it's a problem, but I'm just—"

My eyes lowered to his finger on my lips. My lips burned where the soft padded part of his index finger met the bottom, fuller part of my lips, and all I wanted to do was part my lips and take his finger in. Feel the knuckle of his finger on my tongue and lick it. Taste it. *Suck* it.

"Mia. I know you are seventeen." James pulled away before I could show him my exceptionally amateur sucking skills. I had used those skills once in the back room of Chemistry lab with a classmate, but he came on my expensive new jeans, ruining them, so I never tried it again.

"Come on. Let's go to your bedroom."

I chuckled and ran a hand through my hair. "You don't wait, do you?"

"What's there to wait?"

He unlocked the main door—yes, he even knew the code to our house. That was how much my dad trusted him. *Oh, poor dad. What would he say?* He was with his buddies watching hockey, eating onion rings and thinking his daughter was following the curfew and in bed sound asleep.

"Come on, be quick, Mia. I don't have much time." James ushered me in. "I have early meetings tomorrow."

I'll be in bed for sure. Just for different reasons.

LOOK AT ME AND ANSWER

MIA

I swallowed the lump in my throat and stayed by the front door, which he ordered me to do. He came back with a couple of hand towels after rummaging in the washroom closet. I accepted one of them and started patting my hands and tee-shirt, staring in horror at the sight of my nude bra being glaringly visible through the sheer dark top. The only night I decided to wear something sexy and it embarrasses me. *Great, thanks world.*

"Oh," I let out a soft chuckle when he started patting my wet hair with a towel. "You don't have to."

James glared at me. "You'll get sick. You can't miss your first day of school."

"*High* School." I corrected him, crossing my arms.

His eyes lowered to my arms before snapping at my face as heat crept up his neck. "*Junior* year of high school, Mia. You should take a warm shower before bed and take some cold medicine." He touched my forehead again while I shamelessly admired the way his shirt stretched over his shoulders and tightened over his biceps. *He's so hot.* "Your skin is still hot. Come on, let's get you in bed—"

My eyes blinked at his dark mop of thick, soft, very tuggable hair when he knelt in front of me. *What was he doing down there?*

Then I felt his fingers on my shoes as he removed them. I squeaked, "I-I can do that on my own."

James didn't reply. He simply held my leg and peeled off the wet socks. I shivered, holding on to his muscled shoulders when his hand brushed against the soft skin of my feet, tickling me. When he stood up, his pupils were dilated with an emotion I've never seen on his face... or I was possibly dreaming.

I didn't know what he saw on my face, but he shook his head and snapped, "Come on."

He didn't wait for my reply. He held my wrist and dragged me behind him. James didn't realize that he didn't have to tell me twice or take me. I'd follow him wherever he asked me to.

My heart dropped as soon as we entered my room. I had completely forgotten about the mess of clothes, shoes, makeup, and underwear that I had created while getting ready for the party and leaving it 'for later' before I rushed out.

"Bite my ass," I muttered underneath my breath and shoved the clothes in my closet, almost tripping on a pair of black stilettos. I grunted and heaved, trying to clear my queen-sized princess bed as much as I could.

James must look at my room and think how immature I was. With Korean band posters I outgrew, a *Speed* movie poster because I loved Keanu Reeves, and small polaroids of me and my friends stuck all around the light peach-colored walls.

"I'm sorry." I blushed when he helped me gently remove the band of cherry red push-up bra that was too tiny for my girlies from the corner of the door. "I don't know how it got up there."

"You don't have to apologize. When I was your age, my room looked like an after scene from a war zone."

I bit my lip and nodded, throwing the bra in my dresser and slamming it shut. "So how do you... how do you want to do this?" I asked, looking at my bed with its pink floral duvet cover, nine pillows and two stuffed toys.

I was about to get railed by my crush, who is my father's best-friend slash my soon-to-be-hot-teacher, on the same princess bed he had helped my dad install.

Talk about mid-teen-life-crush crisis.

"Take a shower first."

"*Oh*," I straightened up. I didn't think I smelt that bad, but... okay. "I'll be right—"

A shrill ringtone broke our eye contact. I ignored the tug in my heart when he picked up the call. I could hear a woman's voice on the other end and my heart dropped a little more.

When he ended the call, I knew what he was going to say, so I kept my fake smile ready.

"I'm sorry, Mia. I've to leave soon."

"Of course." I smiled big and wide, nodding way too fast. "No problem."

James walked towards me and I held my breath when his lips came closer and landed on my forehead. "Don't forget to take a hot shower before you tuck yourself in, okay?"

"Of course, James. I'm a big girl now." My smile froze, and I repeated his words in my head. "Wait, what did you just say?"

"I said don't forget to take a hot shower."

"No, after that."

"Tuck yourself in?"

I stared at him and blinked. "You... you wanted to tuck me in?"

"Yes. I said I'm going to tuck you, before we arrived home." He frowned at me and tilted his head. "Are you sure you are okay?"

James never said he wanted to fuck me. He wanted to *tuck* me.

Oh my god, you stupid fucking fool.

"Haha. You wanted to tuck me. *Haha*. Of course. Classic *tuck*ing in. *Ha*."

"You know what?" He pulled out his phone. "On a second note, you don't seem fine. I'll sleep on the couch."

I stopped him from typing out a text to the woman he was going to meet after *tuck*ing me in. I threw cold water on the jealousy that climbed up my heart that wanted him to stay the night, and forced out the awkward words, "It's okay. I'm okay. I'll take a shower and sleep. *Tuck*ing myself."

"Are you sure you don't want me to stay?"

Of course, I want you to stay! I want you to stay with me and gently pat my hair dry after I take a warm shower. I want you to stay and cuddle with me under my floral covers and tell me a story like my mother used to before she passed away. I want you to stay by my side because I'm selfish, and never let you go to warm someone else's bed because I hate it when I'm alone in this damn big house. I want you to stay and wrap your arms around me and tell me it's going to be okay even when it's not going to be.

"Yes, I'm okay!" I smiled and turned around to find my robe so I could shut myself in the shower and he wouldn't have to see the warm tears burning my eyes.

I bit my lip from spilling out my heart when he held up my hand and brushed his lips against my knuckles. The soft touch of his velvety lips sent shivers down my spine, my stomach tightening with nerves as his warm hand cradled mine.

"Call me if you feel sick, okay?"

I nodded, not meeting his eyes because it hurt to see him leave.

His hold tightened on my hand. "Look at me and answer."

"I'll call you if I get sick." I rolled my eyes and met his piercing blue eyes. "Happy now?"

His eyes narrowed at me. "I don't like that tone, young lady. I'm older than you."

"So? You're like eighteen years older. It doesn't matter."

He said underneath his breath, but I caught it, "You don't have to remind me."

Before I could ask what he meant by that, he squeezed my hand and pulled away. "Goodnight, Mia."

I watched his back disappear out of the hallway, going downstairs as I whispered to an empty room, "Goodnight, James."

James

I relaxed my fingers from a tight fist and stared at it.

Soft. Sweet. Innocent.

And your friend's seventeen-year-old daughter.

Shaking my head, I closed my eyes and erased all impure thoughts about a certain doe-eyed vixen with soaking clothes. But it didn't help. Her cherry-scented perfume was all over in the car, and I fucking hated myself for wanting that perfume in every nook and cranny of my car, my clothes, my skin.

"*Hell*," I said to myself, glaring at the two-story house where my sin lived. "You're going to hell for your thoughts, James."

I sighed and messaged her dad and my close friend, Clyde Miller, that his daughter was home safe before shutting down my phone. I had a long night, and I intended to lash out everything on the red-haired woman that had called me.

I would need it. Especially if I was going to torture myself for the next year by teaching a bunch of highschoolers.

PORN STAR NAME

MIA

Waking up with soaked underwear was not ideal. Especially when the reason for the particular soaked underwear was my father's bestfriend, James Fox.

Yes, even his name sounds like a porn star.

Biting my lip, I turned on my back and took a deep breath. I could try it again. Surely, it would be easy after trying to touch myself so many times. Maybe too easy.

You can do it, Mia. Just think about his handsome face, his delicious stern voice, his dark hair and—*fuck, yes, mmm.*

My hands felt small and gentle, cupping my perky breasts. I imagined his large palms—with the *Patek Philippe* on his wrist that I had gifted him on his thirty-fifth birthday—fondling my breasts, the veins on his forearms tensing as he pinches my hard little nipples between his fingers.

A whimper tore out of my lips as my thighs rubbed together, my pussy getting wetter and wetter when I thought about him instructing me how to touch my pussy.

Nonono, in my dream, he calls it *his pussy.*

Yes, *his* pussy. My feminist self really yeets out whenever I have horny thoughts about him.

My eyes flickered to the side, watching my reflection on the closet mirror. My cheeks were flushed, eyes clouded with lust, my palms touching my naked breasts and lowering over my stomach. Caressing the smooth skin and shivering at the image of James in my head.

I parted my legs like he would, keeping his strong hand over my thigh and peeling off my satin shorts with my soaked underwear, mocking me for ruining them with my juices. Oh, how deliciously wicked he'd look with that dark look in his eyes. Even forcing the underwear in my willing mouth when he would go down on me and make me cum with his hot tongue.

Letting out a small moan, I slid my hand inside my underwear, humming when the pad of my finger made contact with my aching clit. The sensitive nub was swollen and buzzing with pleasure as I rubbed it slowly, thinking about his encouraging words in his deep, husky voice.

Just like that, Mia.

That's it.

That's how good girls touch their cunts.

No, no, no, keep going, I didn't tell you to stop.

You are going to cream all over your little fingers for me, hm?

"Mia!"

All my fantasies came crashing down upon hearing the booming voice in the hallway. I removed my hand from my underwear and sat up straight, finding my satin shirt on the floor, which I had discarded last night before sleeping.

No matter what the internet tells you, sleeping naked is a blessing for your body. Especially your breasts.

"Mia, you will be late." My father knocked on the door, making all my fantasies about his best friend vanish.

Taming my hair, I straightened my clothes and opened the door to show him my charming smile. "I won't be late," I said in a cheesy voice, but it seemed too high-pitched. "I will be out of the room in twenty minutes."

"You better, kiddo, if you want me to drop you off. I have an early meeting today."

"Ay, ay, captain!" I closed the door and sighed after locking myself in the bathroom. My cheeks were still flushed and my heart was hammering against my ribs.

If only no one had interrupted me... maybe, just maybe, I would finally know what an orgasm felt like.

"No time to think about it," I muttered to myself and stripped out of my clothes and got in the shower.

I shaved, shampooed and conditioned my shoulder-length hair, and brushed my teeth in the record time of fifteen minutes. I was lucky enough to be enrolled in a private school, so we had to wear a uniform. Crisp white shirt paired with green and black plaid skirt and white socks with shoes of our preference. I altered between my chunky Doc Martens and Mary Janes. Being the first day of my junior year, I opted for Mary Janes.

I wore my favorite jewelry, a dainty heart necklace, and placed it under my shirt. My mom had gifted it to me on the night she died.

Hanging the tie over my shoulder, I ran downstairs with my small backpack in hand and thanking my father for the breakfast.

"Are you ready for the new year, Pumpkin?" he asked, taking the tie from me and expertly tying it for me and handing it back. It was our ritual as I could not, for the life of me, learn how to tie a tie or tie shoelaces. He had tried to teach me, but it was fruitless.

"I am ready, but a little nervous," I answered, eating the strawberries after devouring the eggs. "I have a lot of AP classes and I don't want to fail in any of them."

"You won't," he said and smiled at me. "Even if you do, you know I don't care. Just stay sane and healthy, Pumpkin."

"Yes, Captain."

I applied a little concealer, mascara and lip gloss in the mirror by the hall where mom used to keep her makeup and her little jewelries before going out. I smiled sadly at the picture frame of her by Dad's bedroom that used to be their room before an accident took her away from us.

His arm wrapped around my shoulder and I closed my eyes, breathing in the cozy scent of pumpkin and wood with a lingering whiff of her perfume. I knew he would spritz it on himself, trying to imagine having her back in his arms.

He kissed my head. "She would be very proud to see you today, Mia."

"What?" I chuckled. "Almost late for school?"

He ruffled my hair, and I frowned at him, running my hand through my damp hair and following him into the garage. "You don't have to be nervous. James will be there."

That's the fucking problem, Dad.

"And I told him to take care of you, so you don't have to worry about anything, but maintaining your—"

"Sanity." I ended the sentence for him and closed the car door of the passenger seat. "By the way, Dad… when am I getting my own car again?"

He turned on the ignition of the car and rolled it out of the garage. "When you behave well."

"Which I do."

"*Hmm.*"

"Don't *hmm* me." I sulked in my seat and crossed my arms. "I would love to drive with my friends and go—"

"*Mia.*" He glanced at me, his salt and pepper hair styled the same way since my childhood, his brown eyes stern with lines around them. "If you want to earn a car, you have to show me that you will be responsible for it."

"By doing what, exactly?" I was vexed. "I worked in the diner for three summer vacations and saved up for it, and now you are telling me to be responsible for it. *How?*"

He, of course, didn't reply. I groaned and looked out of the window, wishing Mom was alive and would let me have a car. It wasn't like I couldn't just go in a car shop and buy it since I would become an adult soon, but he was my father, the only person who I was really close to, and I didn't want to do anything without his support.

Or cause him any disappointment.

I looked at the expensive cars that lined up outside the Saint Helena Academy. Sons and daughters of actors, models, and businessmen getting dropped off by the intimidating tall gates. The academy was built on the grounds of the old Saint Helena Palace, with a church on the academic grounds. It was in shambles until a rich billionaire restored the palace and turned it into a private academy for rich kids.

"Have a great day, Pumpkin. Love you!" My father yelled at me as soon as I opened the door and got out, scowling at him.

I quickly showed him my back and walked through the gates, eyeing the intimidating, looming towers of the school. It even had freaking turrets. The palace had three official buildings, and each had their own division for the students and teachers—one for junior high, the biggest one for senior high, and the other one for teachers that also held a gym, an ice rink, and a pool for our sports classes. There was rumored to be an old church somewhere in the trees behind the teachers' building, but it was supposed to be haunted and securities lurked around it as it was off grounds for everyone.

I didn't have a thing for haunted churches in the forest, but my curiosity for it burned me.

My eyes flickered to the vast parking lot where more

luxurious, shiny cars were parked with assigned spots for teachers, and students whose parents donated a large sum to keep the academy running.

"Funny to see you alive and sulking on this fine morning, Mia!" I greeted my friend, Summer Hayes, with a grin as she wrapped her arm around me and walked with me to the hallway. "I finished the entire fantasy series last night, and the descriptions of his dong were just chef's kiss."

"You did not just say dong out loud."

"*Dong*." Summer grinned, "See? I did it again. Oh, look, there's Emma. I will scare her."

I giggled when she ran over to Emma, hugging her from behind and screaming dong in her ear. The poor girl squeaked, making the other people laugh around her for messing with her.

"I hate you," Emma grumbled, rubbing her ear and fixing her beige cardigan. "You are annoying."

Summer poked her tongue out at her. "If you truly hate me, then I won't share the delicious Thai curry my mom cooked for us."

"Summer, you shouldn't yell dong out loud in the hallways or a teacher will scold us." I shuddered, thinking about getting a detention ticket for that. "Or even suspend us. Did you hear what happened to Thomas last year?"

"He skinny dipped in the school pool and Ms. Laxmi found him. Big deal." Emma said as we leaned against her locker, her pastel-colored nails matching her lilac pink purse and the bow pinned on her hair. Her locker was filled with pictures of the three of us, and her and her boyfriend.

"I have heard there's a new faculty joining us this year."

I looked away and found my locker, stashing my books in it and checking my course list again. I did not want to get involved in the talk of James Fox and—

"Yeah, the dude's name is James Fox," Summer said. "It's such a porn star name. Sounds sus, if you ask me."

You and me both.

"Summer." I elbowed her and nodded at Ms. Laxmi, who was walking past us, checking if the students of Saint Helena academy were behaving or not. "You are asking—*no*, begging for a detention slip. Do you want a mic?"

"*Girl,*" she drawled out, sighing and clutching one of her fantasy books in her arms as she went off to la-la land, "The only begging I will do is for his perfectly sized twelve inch do —*semester!*"

She yelled out and straightened up when the dean of our academy gave her a pointed look. I suppressed a shudder when her dark eyes slid to me and Emma. She kept her chin high until she walked away, disappearing between other students.

"Whew, that was close."

I deadpanned, "You think? She will expel you without any thoughts if she had heard you."

She rolled her eyes at me. "Come on, we can't even talk about our fantasies out loud?"

"Sexual fantasies, Summer."

"So? If my mom paid a bit more of a donation, she would forget she ever heard me." She flashed me her teeth and pulled out her notes for the subject.

The bell rang, followed shortly by asking the students to visit the auditorium hall for the first day and get inspired to study more. It was a given that most of us would go to Ivy League universities as soon as we graduate from Saint Helena academy, and get high paying jobs just seeing the name of the academy in our CV.

My mother wanted me to study here and if it wasn't for her, I wouldn't have joined the academy last year… so soon after she died. In a way, I had to thank James and my father for helping me pass the entrance exam for the academy, and fit right in with Emma and Summer.

"We hope you will achieve all your dreams from the Saint Helena academy and let us help you create a better future." The dean ended her speech with a stern voice, eyeing all of us through her sharp glasses.

"My dream is to get fucked by six vampires—"

I elbowed Summer, and held my breath when her eyes slid to our group, glaring directly at Summer, who met her levelling stare.

"See me after your last class, Miss Summer Hayes."

Everyone looked at her, some people chuckling and glaring at her, and a boy outright making an expression of slicing his throat before turning away.

"Don't worry," I said to her when she left the podium. "I will cry on your funereal and play Taylor Swift's songs."

"Har har," she said, flicking her hair over her shoulder. "What's the worst she can do? *Nothing*. I am Summer fucking Hayes."

"Let's go, Mia." Emma wrapped her arm around my elbow. "Summer is still thinking about her five vampire lords and getting railed by them."

"Six vampire lords, Em! *Six*," Summer corrected with a grin. "Keep up!"

I laughed with her and waved at Summer, who had a class in the east wing of the Palace-slash-academy. I wondered why I hadn't seen James during the main assembly. Maybe he was teaching some other class or maybe he would join the next year.

That would be much better. I didn't want to go through the torture of sitting through his lectures, hearing his melodious deep voice and my pussy aching for him. Only if my friends knew how not-so innocent I was, pretending to be a goody two shoes when all I wanted was my father's friend to wrap his hand around my neck and thrust inside me.

Yes. It would be a blessing in disguise if he wouldn't have a class this semester.

But of course, why would God ever listen to a white seventeen-year-old who had sex dreams about her dad's best friend?

"Good morning," James said, prowling into my third class as if he owned the entire building. "I am James Fox and your teacher for Design and Colors."

Oh goodie, this was not good for me or my underwear.

YES, MISTER JAMES?

MIA

His voice rang through the class of twenty teenagers, grabbing our attention and making me squirm in my seat. I tugged at the tie that felt too tight around my neck, trying not to ogle at his tall, broad-shouldered frame. He looked delicious in a fitted crisp white shirt and pants. His shoes were so shiny I wondered if he took an extra hour to polish them. Nah, must have gotten someone else to do it.

But what stood out the most were his glasses. Black frame that perched on his strong nose as his eyes glimmered through them, making me squirm in my seat.

I swallowed the lump in my throat when he answered a small question from a girl, rolling the sleeves of his shirt over his elbow. *Fuck, his arms.* His hands. The watch that I had gifted him glinted in the light streaming in through the open windows.

"Why does his name sound like a porn star?" a guy behind me whispered, and I had to bite the insides of my cheek to stop myself from laughing.

Thank god, I wasn't the only one.

"Is there something you want to share with the class, Matt?" I straightened up, hearing James address the guy behind me. His delicious voice sent shivers down my body, and I had to clench my thighs to suppress myself from looking at him.

"N-no, sir, just surprised to have a new teach for such a small subject."

Uh-oh, he had a death wish.

James chuckled, and I glanced at him when he straightened to his full height, walking out from behind the desk, leaning back on it. He stretched out his long legs in front of him, addressing the class.

"Matt, what do you want to get out of graduating from Saint Helena academy?"

His answer was quick. "I want to get into an Ivy League university, get a degree, maybe get my master's degree and get a job that makes me rich with a big house and a hot girlfriend—"

"I'll stop you right there." Our teacher smiled, students snickering with him. "Who else wants to get rich and live in a big house as Matt put it?"

Everyone raised their arms. Everyone except one. I rolled my eyes when he pointed out Emma.

"And your reason miss…"

"Emma," she answered, crossing her arms and leaning back on the chair. "I already live in a mansion and I don't need to get rich, Mister Fox. I *am* rich."

"Of course," he pursed his lips and got back on the topic. "As most of you want to get rich, earn a lot of money, you will also either buy or build luxurious houses, apartments or buildings for your clients. But before that, you need to learn how space and design works."

"That sounds so boring."

He nodded at the girl who said it, "It does, but in the

future you will thank me for teaching you how to design. So stop whining and look over the material I hand you."

I leaned down to take out my notes from my backpack when I heard his voice—much closer to me, startling me out of the stupor from his introduction.

"Miss Miller?"

My heartbeat stuttered as I eyed his polished shoes and my eyes drifted over his perfectly ironed slacks, his belt, the buttons of his shirt, his delectable adam's-apple, the scruff on his sharp jaw, kissable lips, and strong nose to his dark green eyes.

"Y-yes?" I asked, blinking at him. "Yes, Mister James?"

"Can you share these notes with your classmates?"

I'll do anything you ask me to if you keep looking at me like that.

He kept a bundle of spiral notes on my desk, but I was too busy ogling the short lock of hair that was falling right over his left brow, making him look much more desirable. I wanted to lean closer and tuck it away.

Clearing my throat, I stood up, my chair squeaking behind me as I held the notes closer and nodded quickly, avoiding his eyes but memorizing his bare forearm—*ohmygod he has veins on his hands and arms*—and turned around to hand over the notes before I lean closer to him in front of all my classmates.

That would be a pretty embarrassing thing to do on the first day of school.

I can do that on the last day of school.

MIA, GET YOUR HEAD OUT OF THE GUTTER—

"Is there some problem, Miss Miller?"

Yes, you see I have been getting wet dreams about you for a while, and you were the reason I was being so squirmy right now because my panties were soaked just hearing you say a few things about the class, wearing THOSE pants that make your ass looks so... *delectable*.

Holding back my shiver, I continued sharing the notes and smiled at him, "No problem, Sir."

James

Just one look at her flushed cheeks and glazed hazel-green eyes, I knew what dirty little Mia was thinking about that made her squirm every few seconds on her chair. It was distracting to see her cross and uncross her legs with her plaid skirt lowering on her thigh. It made me clench my fingers in a fist from scolding her, because her male classmates couldn't keep their eyes from the revealing skin.

But I had promised to be a good teacher, a better friend to Clyde, and signed the contract, so insistent on teaching young minds the art of design.

No matter how jealous I was, no matter how tempting the distraction was, no matter how my hands were itching to slip under her skirt, and scold her for ruining her underwear—it was *wrong*.

She was seventeen years old, and even worse, my friend's daughter.

Clyde Miller was one of my first clients when I had joined the world of design as an intern. He must have seen potential in me. That was the only reason he helped me, even loaned me money out of his own pocket when I couldn't afford to buy anything else than eggs or rice. Not to mention he was stubbornly kind towards me since that night.

So I had made the wise decision of sticking to teaching and focusing on answering the questions students had. Even when she raised her hand, tucking a dark stray lock behind her ear and asked me about the three-point-perspective in her sweet voice.

Thankfully, the bell rang announcing the period was over, and it was amusing to see how everyone started packing their bags, boys bumping my fists as if I was one of them, before walking out of the class and hooting.

Ah, reminds me how loud I was as a teenager.

"Miss Miller," I called her as she walked past my desk with her friend, who narrowed her eyes at me. She came from old money. I could tell from one look at her, but I couldn't give a shit. "I thought you already knew about all three perspectives."

Mia's eyes widened a little before she faced me with an innocent expression on her face, her notes in her hands. "I know, but I wanted to test you, Mister Fox. Hope you have a wonderful first day at Saint Helena Academy."

I kept my eyes on her as she walked away with her friend, laughing about something and leaving me alone in the class with a pang of arousal and guilt.

Closing my eyes, I took a deep breath and erased the filthy, corrupting thoughts from my head. They were just that, *thoughts*.

Empty desires and nothing more.

I got a ping on my phone and checked the message. I exhaled sharply, seeing a text from Clyde Miller.

> Good luck on your first day of teaching! As Mia would say, 'Go and get some.'

>> hank you, but for the love of God, please never ever repeat—or type that sentence again.

> Yeet

>> -_-

> XD Gottem

> I have a couple more classes, so see you around, old man.

> Ay, don't forget about today's dinner!

My brows furrowed, and I had to check my calendar's app to see that I had blocked my evening with 'Dinner @ Miller's House - Gift' from four to eight in the evening.

Shit, I have to get the gifts, too.

Having dinner with them every other week or every month had started since I met Clyde, but I had avoided going to his house. It stopped briefly over a few years when I went abroad to further my knowledge about Green engineering and working on a few projects, but we had started our dinner rituals again since last year. I'd either visit them or they would visit my house. Gifting was optional, but we gladly appreciated alcohol and books with some sort of dessert, as both Clyde and his daughter had an extremely sweet tooth.

My phone vibrated in my hand, and I glanced at the upcoming message from him.

> By the lack of your response, either your class has started, or you forgot about the dinner.

> I didn't exactly forget about it. I'll be there, don't worry.

After all, I have never missed a single dinner or lunch with them.

* * *

THE FIRST DAY of school ended with a small email from the dean, who wanted to make sure we were all on our best behaviors and showing enthusiasm for the year.

As much as I had fun teaching students about design, space, and colors, I missed being in my private office. The solitude and quietness that came with drafting on sheets, the rough but comfortable sound of lead pencil drifting through the paper, and my loud head brimming with ideas to turn the dream of my clients into a reality.

But I was teaching, sharing my secrets with young minds, and I knew it would help them in their future. I just had to teach until the contract ends.

Packing my notes in the briefcase, I closed the lights in the office that the school had offered me. It was a comfortable room with a couch, desk and chairs, bookshelves, a little storage room and even a bathroom. Considering it was a private academy, no wonder they offered such luxuries to teachers as well, with their high pay.

I remembered my public school and how tiny the teachers' office was, and they didn't have their own office or an entire building to themselves. You'd have to go to the ground floor and hope that the teacher wasn't busy to help you with your doubts.

"James."

I paused and looked at the dark hair of the familiar figure. Removing my black-framed glasses, I stood beside her. "What are you doing here, Mia?"

From what I knew after the teacher's orientation, students rarely crossed over to the teachers' building unless it was really important. My eyes zeroed in on her face, her arms and legs. Not noticing any bruise, I tilted my head, "Are you in trouble?"

Get Tempting Teacher to read the sweet, forbidden

romance of Mia and James.

PREVIEW OF DIRTY WILD SULTAN

NASRIN

Zain chuckled, his laugh devoid of any humor making me shudder. He leaned closer and my eyes widened when his lips went past mine to press against my ear as he whispered, "I don't want to know why you think so lowly of me but I assure you, future *wife*..." A slither of pleasure rolled over my spine hearing his rumbling velvety voice, his lips brushing over the shell of my ear, "That you would be the one begging me to touch you."

He was so right, he had no idea.

I would beg. For him. *Only* him.

My eyes were glazed when they roved over his powerful, lean body, the muscles on his biceps moving when he leaned back on the stool. I pressed my teeth on my bottom lip, the air around us thickening with the steam, exotic oil, his musky cologne.

I met his eyes. "Then I beg you to touch me, Zain." I swallowed the lump in my throat and added in a soft whisper, "Please."

His eyes widened a little with shock, and something darker coursed through them. My heart thudded loudly when I realised what it was. Pure lust. Desire. If I could move back in the bath, I would, because his gaze turned predatory, and I felt like his prey. Naked in the bath, while he was covered in clothes.

I watched when he unbuttoned the top two buttons of his dark shirt, revealing the tan skin underneath. My tongue seeped out to wet my lips. A hint of a smirk grazed his lush lips when he said,

"Spread your legs and show me your cunt, Princess."

PREVIEW OF DON'T DATE YOUR BEST FRIEND

KIARA

"If you don't want to kiss me then . . . let's swim."

"Yeah, sure."

"Naked."

"*What?*"

"I always wanted to try skinny dipping." I pursed my lips and said, "And I really want to get out of these clothes."

When I thought about it, I wasn't feeling self-conscious about my body when it came to him. Yes, he had seen in me in bikinis and accidentally walking in when I was busy writing something on my Post-it in my underwear and bra. But I was never self-conscious about what he would think of me or my body. I did have stretch marks, but I wasn't uncomfortable about them. What I was most worried about was *myself*. If he got naked and my hormones spiked up, I didn't know if I would control myself and not jump on him.

Gosh, I sounded so bad in my head. Not to mention, my best friend would be the first guy I would ever see naked. *Way to go, Kiara.*

His voice was strained when he said, "What if someone catches *you* . . . me, both?"

I moved my damp hair over my shoulder. "We will be in the pool, Ethan. And no one can see us from the living room." I smirked when I said, "Unless you want to watch me while I swim, you can stay here."

The thought of Ethan watching me with his intense green-blue eyes while I was swimming naked in the pool sent a delicious shiver down my core.

His eyes darkened and he looked away, probably thinking the same when I noticed red blush creeping up his neck and making his ears and cheeks flush. *Cute.*

I prodded, "Come on, Ethan. Don't be a chicken . . ."

"*Fine.*"

He stood up, his tall frame towering me. I forgot how to breathe when his dark eyes seared me, slowly trailing down my body as if he had all the time in the world. His voice was rough when he said, "Remove that sweater first."

I raised my eyebrow at the sudden change in his demeanour.

Ethan said, "You have an extra piece of clothing than me."

I grinned. "Who said I was wearing any underwear?"

I loved the way his pupils widened in shock, surprise and then they were clouded by scorching desire. Biting my lips, I whispered, "I was messing with you."

Holding the hem of the sweater, I tugged it up and removed it. I straightened my damp hair and shivered. But it wasn't because of the cold air.

His eyes averted down my breasts, which were barely covered by the ivory lace bralette. As it was wet, he could easily notice my hardened nubs, which were begging for his attention.

We were crossing a dangerous line right now. And I knew neither one of us wanted to step back.

"Your turn," I managed to whisper.

EXCLUSIVE CONTENT

Want more exclusive content? You can sign up for Mahi's Patreon to read exclusive one-shots!

As a supporter, you get access to early drafts, exclusive VIP content, deleted scenes, deleted chapters, cat pictures and YOUR NAME in the Acknowledgements of my books.

www.patreon.com/mahimistry

ALSO BY MAHI MISTRY

Have you read them all?

Dominating Desires Series

Twisted Therapist: Brother's Best Friend Age Gap Romance

Tempting Teacher: Student Teacher/Dad's Best Friend Age Gap Romance

Bossy Bodyguard: Bodyguard/ Ex's Dad Age Gap Romance

Billionaire Boss: Sister's Best Friend Age Gap Romance

Bratty Badboys: Single Mom, Biker, Ex-Boyfriend's Mom, MMF, Reverse Age Gap Romance

Sinful Suit: Billionaire Lawyer Age Gap Romance

Alluring Rulers of Azmia Series

Dirty Wild Sultan

Filthy Hot Prince

Tempting Rebel Princess

Charming Handsome Sheikh

Alluring Rulers of Azmia Complete Series Books 1-4

The Unfolding Duet

Don't Date Your Best Friend: Best Friends to Lovers

Don't Date Your Ex Best Friend: Second Chance Best Friends to Lovers

The Unfolding Duet Books 1-2

Scan to easily access all of my books:

ACKNOWLEDGMENTS

Thank you so much for reading Twisted Therapist.

Thank you to all my beta readers, editor, proofreader, arc readers, bloggers and book lovers, bookstragramers, I couldn't have done this without you. Especially Anastasia Ant. You're a precious gem and I'm so honoured you to have you as my dear reader and friend.

Thank you to everyone who accepted the ARC edition of this book and helped me share this book with the world.

If you enjoyed reading this book, please don't forget to leave a review. I would really appreciate it. It helps find more readers like you and they are very important for authors!

ABOUT THE AUTHOR

Mahi Mistry has been writing since she was in middle school. Soon, she fell in love with writing passionate, steamy romances. Her stories have elements of humor, suspense and character development. Mahi's main purpose in her life is to make one person happy every day, even if that is a stranger reading her book and rooting for the main couple or her cats by giving them extra treats.

She enjoys simple things in life, like spending time with her family and friends, cuddling with her cats, reading and writing drool-worthy characters while sipping on hot chocolate from the wineglass to validate herself that she is actually an adult. She is an avid reader of fantasy, romance and thriller books and thinks writing about yourself in third person is atrocious. She firmly believes that cats rule the world.

www.mahimistry.com

www.ingramcontent.com/pod-product-compliance
Lightning Source LLC
LaVergne TN
LVHW041949070526
838199LV00051BA/2956